FLEA MARKET FELONY

The Mattie and Mo Mysteries

TRICIA L. SANDERS

DEDICATION

This book, this series is dedicated to Ray.
Always in my heart.

ACKNOWLEDGMENTS

The idea for this book started with a real rescue dog named Max. Max was almost eight when he came into our lives. He arrived with a long list of animal control violations, escapes from foster homes, and a personality deemed unfit for society. Enter my daughter who had never met a dog she didn't fall in love with. She took Max in temporarily the weekend before he was scheduled to be sent to doggie heaven or hell as the case may be. Needless to say, he never returned to the shelter to face his fate. Instead, he became a pampered family member, big brother to rambunctious Matisse, and alpha dog in the Sanders' household. And the best darn rescue dog ever.

Max lived another ten years before crossing the rainbow bridge at the age of eighteen. Thank you to my daughter, Amy Sanders, for bringing Maxwell Smarticus into our lives.

Thanks to several readers who helped name characters and locations. Janice Busby suggested Oldies but Goodies RV Park and Flea Market. Sharon Frank suggested Sarge. Jennifer Jones suggested Calla Lily, Cal for short. Robyn Krontz provided Olive's name, and Jeannie Murphy recommended the name Ruby. Thanks ladies! I hope I did your names justice.

Thanks to my ARC team for taking the time to read Mattie and Mo's story before it was released into the wild. Barb Nickelson, Sue Stoner, Jan Tomalis, Michelle Ewing, Jen Mallette, Laura Reading, Barb Schmidt, Lee Dunn, Regina de los Reyes, Cathy Lundberg, Susan Rae Buck, Amy Newman Connolley, Christine Walker, Dee Doub, Sherry Legan, Lori Boness Caswell, Mary Ingmire, Maggie Herrel, Meg Gustafson, Kara Marks, and Jerri Cachero, you ladies are appreciated so much.

As always, kudos to the Lit Ladies. Sarah Patsaros, Brandi Schmidt, Camille Subramaniam, Margo Dill, and Grace Malinee are my go-to girls for critiquing, brainstorming, and sprinting.

Special thanks to Cayce Berryman at Kingsman Editing Service for her keen eye and witty comments.

A big thank you to Mariah Sinclair for my cover.

CHAPTER ONE

As we drove the winding road, through a forest of tall oaks and views of the glistening lake with sailboats bobbing like ducks on a pond, my hopes for a perfect vacation soared. A week alone with my husband and no distractions sent naughty ideas scampering through my brain.

Mo stopped the RV at the entrance to the Oldies but Goodies RV Park and Flea Market.

All thoughts of hanky-panky screeched to a halt. "Are you sure this is the right place?" An old tire lay propped against a wooden sign hanging from frayed ropes, threatening to disintegrate at any moment. I sat up and stared at the dilapidated sign, my cheerful mood turning sour. "It looks sketchy." And sketchy was being generous.

Mo pulled a packet from over the visor and thumbed through the papers. "Oldies but Goodies RV Park and Flea Market. This is the place."

"How much research did you do? This is one step up from the county dump."

"Mattie, don't be so judgmental. I know how much you and Lizbeth like to go browsing at flea markets. I thought you'd enjoy it." Mo shifted to drive and pulled into the parking lot.

My best friend and I loved to browse flea markets, but Lizbeth wasn't here and flea marketing by myself didn't sound fun. And flea marketing with Mo sounded even less fun. He had recently retired as police chief of our tiny town of Pine Grove. To be fair, I had been begging him for two years to retire, but I never dreamed we'd spend our retirement in an RV.

The RV was the last gift from my late stepfather, Lazy Lou. When Mo retired, even though I had reservations about RVing, how could I say no? This was our first trip in the new motor home. From the looks of this place, it could be our last. I missed Lizbeth. I didn't know how I would get through an entire summer not seeing her.

"Nothing about this place screams fun, and besides, how much fun can it be? It's not like you'll be around. Not with all the fishing equipment you brought."

"Did you see that lake? It's calling my name. *Mo. Mo.*" He laughed and slapped the steering wheel. "I crack myself up."

"More like you're a crackpot." I stuck out my tongue.

He reached over and squeezed my knee. "We can have lots of fun, if you know what I mean." He winked, and his eyebrows wiggled like two fuzzy gray caterpillars.

I laughed and jostled his hand. "Don't distract me."

"We're only here a week. Then we head back home." Mo parked the forty-foot, Class A motor home in front of a blue stucco A-frame building that looked like it had at one time housed a gas station. Fading fish painted every color under the rainbow swam a motionless path around the building. A sign over the door declared it the office of the Oldies but Goodies RV Park and Flea Market. Fake topiaries of boxwood stood sentry on either side of the glass door.

"Yeah, we're only home a week before we head out for the rest of the summer. Yippee," I grumbled. Mo had picked this campground because it was next to one of the largest lakes in our home state of Missouri. He presumed the flea market would be an added benefit to keep me busy.

"I thought you were excited about starting this next chapter. You've been on my case to retire so we could travel." Mo's normally jovial grin sagged into a frown. "If you don't want to do this, I wish you had let me know before we rented out the house for the summer. We're kind of stuck now."

The defeat on my husband's face tore a hole in my heart.

"You're right. Don't worry, I'll snap out of it. Promise." We had leased our house to a young couple who had lost theirs in a fire and needed a place to live while they rebuilt. That had been my idea, not Mo's. I had started this whole escapade. Now I was the one having second thoughts.

When Mo retired, I had been ecstatic, but I hadn't thought about what it meant to leave our home and friends. By travel, I had meant a week in Florida, or a week in Texas, or a week in Maine staying in a quaint bed-and-breakfast with meals in restaurants and maid service—not three months in a home on wheels where I was the maid and cook. And certainly not a whole summer.

"You'll see Lizbeth when we go back. We'll set up in their driveway, and the two of you can blabber all night for seven nights. Then when we get to Wisconsin, you can video chat or text or whatever it is you do on that phone."

Our rescue dog, Max, stirred in the back and stuck his nose between our seats. "I'm going to leash him up and take him for a walk while you check in."

Mo squeezed my knee tighter. "Hon, it'll be okay. This place looks a little rough around the edges, but the ratings were good. The reviews bragged about how welcoming everyone is."

"We'll see." I snorted, unbuckled my seat belt, and felt around the back of the seat for Max's leash. Instead of finding the leash, a cold, wet nose nudged my hand. "Hey, Max," I said to the gray-muzzled, seventy-pound black Labrador we rescued last Christmas.

Mo handed me the leash. "Give it one night. If you're still not convinced by this time tomorrow, we can head back. Lizbeth and Donny won't mind putting us up an extra week."

"Deal," I said, wrangling the dog out the door. "Twenty-four hours." I made a show of checking the fitness tracker strapped to my wrist. "Four thirty on the dot."

Mo followed me out the door and kissed my cheek. "That's my girl."

I stretched and looked around, catching a glimpse of the lake beyond the office. I squinted and the office blurred. Maybe if I changed my perspective, I could do this for a week. Max tugged his leash, and the building came back into focus.

"Come on, boy," I said.

Max sniffed every tree, bush, and blade of grass before finding the perfect spot to do his business. On the way back to the RV, I spotted a red-haired woman wearing a pair of bun-hugging shorts and a halter top. She entered the office with a tiny dachshund at her heels. I found a shady place next to the RV, filled a bowl with water for Max, and secured his leash.

"You stay here and be good. I'll be right back." He made two circles and curled up in the shaded grass. "Good doggo. If you see a squirrel, ignore it." No matter how well behaved he was, all it took was a stray cat or an errant squirrel to divert his attention. I handed him a treat and headed inside.

～

"You'll be in space eighteen. Go down this lane, turn left after the golf cart crossing, and you're the second spot on the left." A petite white-haired woman, about my age, handed Mo a brochure. A name tag pinned to a scoop-neck flowered tee announced her as Olive—Manager.

"Here's a map and a calendar of activities. Yoga every morning except Sunday at seven a.m. Pool's open until ten every night. Keep your dog leashed at all times, and make sure you pick up after him. Flea market is open tomorrow and Sunday from eight to eight, and a half day on Wednesday. Lots of bargains. Some vendors are open tonight, but only for park residents and guests. If you need anything else, just ask. I'm Olive." A network of soft lines etched her friendly face.

The woman in the skimpy outfit sidled up to Mo—a little too close. Her dog sniffed at Mo's ankles. "Or you could ask me. I'm a permanent resident, so I know my way around." She chuckled and stuck her hand out. "I'm Calla Lily, but everyone calls me Cal. I'm the social director here."

I stared at her. The woman I'd seen from behind had looked much younger, but face-to-face I determined the years had left their mark on Calla Lily. Deep crow's feet clawed at the corners of her eyes. Brackets surrounded her mouth, giving her the look of a marionette. She was every bit of seventy-five, maybe older. The color of her hair did not exist in any form in nature except maybe the scarlet macaw I'd seen at our local zoo.

"Quit making a nuisance of yourself, Cal," Olive said between clenched teeth. "Leave Mr. Modesky alone."

My thoughts exactly.

"And you are not the social director," Olive added with a force that belied her tiny frame. "Social distracter is more like it. Go on. Let my customers be." She made a shooing motion.

Mo grinned like the Cheshire Cat. "Oh, she's fine." He took Cal's hand and shook it. A little too long for my comfort.

I cleared my throat and gave her what I hoped was a dismissive look before turning my attention to Mo. "Are we ready?"

Mo dropped her hand. "Sure thing, hon." He handed me the brochure. "I have all the information we need."

"I bet you do," I said.

"Stop by my place tonight. I can give you the grand tour." Cal ignored me and winked at Mo. "Then maybe we can take a dip in the pool." She picked up her dog, who had wrapped his leash around her leg.

I stepped between her and Mo. "He doesn't swim. And with this map, we can find everything we need. And I do mean everything."

Olive made a clicking noise with her tongue. "Cal, leave the Modeskys alone."

"I'm in the corner unit three streets down on the right. You can't miss it. I have Chinese lanterns hanging from the porch. Stop by for that tour and a swimming lesson." Cal fluffed her fake-as-a-three-dollar-bill hair, flounced across the room, and slammed the rickety screen door behind her.

Olive blew out a breath. "She will be the death of me. You'd think after a certain age, her hormones would dry up and wither away. Instead, she's like a sex-starved sailor. You'd do well to keep an eye out for her and her twin sister, Ruby. They'll chase anything wearing pants, and they aren't picky. No offense, Mr. Modesky."

Mo still stared out the door as Cal sashayed across the parking lot.

I jabbed him in the ribs.

"Huh?" Mo said.

"Put your tongue back in your mouth. She's got to be ten years older than you," I said.

"Cal and Ruby turn seventy-eight next week," Olive said. "Not that it's slowed them down."

"Are you serious? She's got some nerve blatantly coming on to my husband while strutting around like a teenager." I winced, wondering how my sags and bags would look in a halter top.

"She swims laps, jogs five miles a day, and she and Ruby take turns running our yoga class. All that when she's not riding her bike." Olive handed Mo his credit card and the receipt.

"No wonder she looks so good." Mo's face turned red. "Did I say that out loud?"

"Yes, you did," I said.

"I meant fit," Mo said. "You know. In shape."

I looked down at my belly pooch and the one threatening to spill over Mo's belt. Mo and I had been a little careless with our diet and exercise since he'd retired. Maybe now was the time to think about getting into shape, especially if we'd be running into people like Cal in these campgrounds. "Quit while you're ahead, lover boy." I wondered if Mo would be interested in bike riding. That would keep him occupied and provide a great opportunity for both of us to get some much-needed exercise.

Olive reached over and touched my arm. "She will try anything to get a man's attention. Anything. Married or single—it doesn't matter to her. Between you and me, keep a tight leash on your man."

"Hey, I'm standing right here," Mo said.

"Just sayin'. She has no scruples. And when she's not on the prowl, Ruby is. Cal's current obsession is Sarge, but that won't stop her from testing the waters with a new man."

"She'd better watch herself. I don't take kindly to anyone messing with Mo." I didn't worry about him cheating. He'd had his share of opportunities in our forty-plus years of marriage, but he'd never once given me a reason to worry. I grabbed his arm. "Come on, hound dog, let's go find our spot."

Mo leaned in and kissed my cheek. "No woman holds a candle to you, hon."

"You got that right, and you'd best remember that,

because that candle could burn you to a crisp." I laughed and made a sizzling sound.

"Don't underestimate Cal." Olive flipped the CLOSED sign into place and followed us out the door.

"Cal better not underestimate me," I said.

CHAPTER TWO

I heard voices outside while I put away the groceries we'd purchased earlier. Mo had taken Max outside and was hooking up outside lines for the RV. I opened a window to have a listen. Our spot had a large concrete patio next to a picnic table, a barbecue grill, and all the hookups we needed for our motor home. Mo had set out our lawn chairs and the folding side tables we'd brought. We loved having our morning coffee and tea outside. He'd even put a spare dog bed outside so Max would not be lying directly on the concrete.

"Did you say something?" I yelled out the window.

The woman from the office, Cal, lounged on the picnic table next to where Mo was hooking up the power. She was yapping her fool head off. I let the curtain fall aside and went out the door.

"What's going on?" I stomped down the metal steps and across the patio to the table.

Mo looked up, innocence written all over his face. "She brought a cherry pie for dessert. Wasn't that nice?"

I stared down at the store-bought pie. It wasn't in my nature to be jealous or rude, but this woman was intentionally pushing my buttons, and I wasn't in the mood to pretend she wasn't.

"Thanks." I pushed the pie across the table. "That *was* nice, but we're both watching our calories."

Her eyes moved to my middle, and a snarky grin appeared on her face. The curtain in the neighboring RV opened.

"Who's watching their ca—" Mo stood and turned around. When he saw me with my hands on my hips, he patted his belly. "She's right. We both need to take off a few pounds."

I cut him a withering glance and sucked in my stomach.

"Guess I better get back to work." Mo took the hint. He picked up a tool and moved to the rear of the RV, leaving me to deal with our unwanted guest.

"You sure you don't want a little cherry pie? I baked it myself just for you." Sweetness dripped from her mouth.

I took a step closer. My pulse pounded at my temples. "Right, we've been here all of ten minutes and you rushed home and baked a pie? You need to tell me your secret. Wait, I already know. I bought that same one for my card group last month. Now take your pie and leave." My voice came out high and shrill, but I recognized the pie as one straight from the nearest grocery store freezer case. Did she think my husband was desperate enough to fall for a septuagenarian with a frozen pie?

A couple walking their dog stopped and stared. I wondered if the woman had encountered a similar experience with Cal.

"Well, you don't have to get your feathers all ruffled. Just trying to be neighborly." Cal scooted off the table.

For a minute, nagging fingers of guilt gripped me. I always made friends with everyone. My women's group back home had voted me hospitality chair, for Pete's sake. The minute passed, and the guilt disappeared. Red, hot anger remained. "You're wasting your time," I said. "Peddle your pie elsewhere."

Cal winked and brushed my shoulder as she walked past me. "You can't stop him from looking."

My last nerve snapped. "You didn't just say that." Before I could stop myself, I grabbed the pie and hurled it at her. "Get out of here. If you come back, you'll get more than you bargained for." I missed her by a couple of feet, but it felt good seeing her pie in shambles on the ground. Too good. I didn't know what I'd do if she persisted, but I had no intention of standing back and watching her make a play for my husband.

Mo rushed over and put his arm around me. "Take it easy, hon."

When Cal approached the couple in the street, the man gave her a brief wave. The wife slugged him on the shoulder and said something I couldn't hear. Cal kept walking but doubled down on the swing in her hips.

"Did you even hear what she said?" My outburst had left me angry and unsettled. It wasn't like me to snap, but that woman had shaken my cage. Mo always said I was sassy, but never once had I been mean to someone—not intentionally. Not unless they deserved it, anyway.

Mo shrugged. "No."

"Of course you didn't."

"Mattie, another woman is the last thing on my mind. Trust me, you're all the woman I can handle, and after all these years, I'm sure not looking for another one. She's just trying to get a reaction. Turn on your Mattie charm. If you make friends, who knows, you might find a new pal, and she might think twice about being flirty. She's just looking for attention. Maybe what she needs is a friend."

I scoffed. "You are so clueless. I'm going to take Max for a walk."

"Think about what I said, hon," Mo called as Max and I

headed to the flea market. I had no desire to shop, but I also didn't want to hang around and listen to Mo's opinion of Cal. The woman was trouble with a capital *T*. I had a best friend. One who would never make a move on my husband. I sure didn't want one with a reputation as a man chaser.

We walked up and down the four mostly empty streets on our side of the RV park. The lack of RVs shouldn't have surprised me considering the shabbiness of the place. When we came to the end of the last street, Max and I headed down the main road to where it dead-ended in a vast parking lot. Row after row of brightly painted squares marked spaces for booths. Over the entire lot, only about twenty spots had canopies or tents. The rest sat empty. I hoped more vendors would arrive tomorrow. Max and I strolled through the area admiring the scant offerings.

When I saw a display of pocketknives, I stopped. A distinguished silver-haired gentleman wearing an army-green T-shirt and camouflage shorts manned this booth. He had to be at least eighty. It appeared Oldies but Goodies RV Park and Flea Market had been aptly named. I had yet to meet anyone under the age of sixty.

He came around to the front of the table. "Name's Sterling Gray Thorne, but everyone calls me Sarge. Get it?"

"Get what?" I asked.

"My nickname."

"Oh, the army gear. Guess you were a sergeant in the military," I said, scanning the selection of knives displayed in a velvet-lined case.

"Good guess, but no. It's my initials. S-G-T. Short for sergeant. That's why everyone calls me Sarge."

I looked up. "Ha! That's a good one. I'm Mattie, short for Martha." This must be the gentleman Olive said Cal was interested in. I could see why. His eyes were bright blue with crinkly lines at the corners, and for an old guy, he was in excellent shape—tall, lean, and tanned. He reminded me of Paul Newman in his older years.

"Are you interested in a knife?"

"Yes, for my husband," I said.

"I have a great selection." He pulled out another tray and set it on the table. "Let me unlock that for you. Got a guy down in Florida who makes these for me. No two are alike—guaranteed. If you find a duplicate, I'll give you your money back and you keep the knife." After he unlocked the case, he lifted the lid.

I selected one with an eagle carved into the handle. Mo had an affinity for pocketknives and eagles. This would make a great "I know I was snotty" gift. Mo and I did that occasionally when we knew we'd been grouchy to the other one, usually accompanying the gift with a witty card to break the tension. I wasn't ready to break the tension that much. "What's the price?"

"They retail for fifty, but I sell them for forty."

I turned the knife over and pulled open the blade, looking for a brand. There was none. The blade locked into place, which I knew Mo liked. "This one is nice," I said.

"I have a better quality one but not one with an eagle. This is a good everyday carry knife. If you travel a lot, he'll like the smaller blade. Larger ones can get you into trouble with the law in some states. They don't sharpen as nicely as the better ones, but they keep a decent edge."

"I'll give you twenty for it," I said, proud of myself for my bargaining prowess.

"Well . . ." He laughed. "You drive a hard bargain. I can do twenty-five each, if you buy two."

I thought for a minute. One would make a nice Christmas present for my son-in-law, and I'd have another gift out of the way.

"Now look who's driving the hard bargain." I handed him

my credit card. "Deal." I reached into the tray and selected one with a carved elk.

While he was processing my card, loud voices erupted in the next booth.

"I already have a jewelry booth!" a female voice yelled. "You can't set up a competing booth. It's against the rules."

"Who says?" another female screamed.

Sarge handed me my card and the knives. "Oh, Lord, we got another cat fight on our hands."

"Sounds serious," I said.

"That's Cal and Sandi. They have this same argument every time Sandi sets up her booth. You'd think one or the other would give up. But no, they go at it like two queen bees. It's a surprise one of them hasn't killed the other."

The voices drifted over, louder this time. "I say. That's who. I've had my booth for years, and no newcomer is going to come in and upstage me with cheap trinkets from who knows where," the first voice hollered.

"That would be Cal," Sarge whispered. "Gets her panties in a twist every time Sandi or anyone sets up a booth. She's been here longer than most of us and thinks it's her place to weed out the competition."

"Who are you calling a newcomer? I've been coming here almost as long as you. Now, step away and get your nose out of my business," the other woman said.

"That's Sandi. She and her husband pulled their rig in two days ago. They're temps, but they come down so often, everyone knows them. She and Cal have already had a couple of dustups. Now this." He shook his head. "Don't know why decent folk can't just get along."

"I said get out of my booth and leave me alone. I've had it with you, Cal. If you don't leave me and my husband alone, you'll have more to worry about than my little jewelry booth," Sandi said. "Get out, before I lose my patience."

"The womenfolk around here got nothing better to do than raise a fuss. Present company excluded, of course."

Max whined.

"It's fixing to get nasty. You might want to get gone before the merchandise starts flying." Sarge moved a large ceramic flowerpot from the side of his booth that adjoined Sandi's.

"Are you seri—"

A carton sailed past me and landed on the ground next to Max. He yelped and jerked at his leash.

"Yeah, we'll be moving along." I raised my bag with the knives and shook it. "Thanks!"

Max and I continued down the row until the angry voices faded. I stopped at a booth with toys for children and picked out a wooden truck for my grandson. Next, a booth with purses and leather goods caught my eye. A sign on the table showed the owner would be back in fifteen minutes. Instead of hanging around, I made a mental note to stop by tomorrow. A purse would make a splendid gift for Lizbeth.

I took the long way back, bypassing the drama. Max and I checked the few remaining booths along the way and made a pass by the swimming pool, which looked inviting. I could read by the pool, maybe even get in some water aerobics this week since browsing the flea market wouldn't take up much time.

Max slowed down and lagged, showing his age and that he'd had enough walking. Instead of taking the road, we took a shortcut through a little park we'd passed earlier. I heard the muffled sound of crying and saw Cal crouched over on a bench, which made me realize that she truly managed to make herself found all over this place. I refused to feel sorry for her and detoured through a vacant RV spot to the safety of my home away from home.

Mo had set plates and utensils on the picnic table. He stood at the grill tending bratwurst and foil-wrapped corn on the cob. He'd also strung up the solar lights that our friends had given us as a bon voyage gift. I couldn't wait for the sun to set to see how they twinkled. I hurried inside, threw together a salad, and joined him for dinner. While we ate, I told him about the outburst I'd overheard between Cal and the woman in the booth next to Sarge.

Mo swiped his corn through a puddle of butter. "I'm telling you, Mattie. The woman needs a friend."

"And you want me to be that friend, correct?"

"Would it hurt to try?"

"Mo Modesky, you're a kind man. Naïve, but kind."

"*Hmpf*," Mo grumbled. "You know I'm right. You just won't admit it."

"We can agree to disagree." I remembered the knife I'd bought to make peace for our earlier disagreement. A lesser woman would have left it in the bag. Not me. I went inside, grabbed the knife, and set it on the picnic table in front of Mo. "Here. Don't say I never gave you anything. And don't read anything into it. I got it cheap. I bought one for Michael. I'm going to get one for Donny too. And while I'm at it, I'm going to do a little shopping for me and Lizbeth. Oh, and I can get Christmas presents for the girls." Take that, Mo Modesky.

Mo shook his head. "I may be sorry I picked this place. Don't break the bank with all your shopping."

"Your idea to come here, not mine. Suffer the consequences. Besides, you know how hard Donny and Lizbeth are to buy for. If I can get their gifts early, it takes the pressure off."

Donny and Lizbeth were not only our neighbors, but our best friends. Donny was the director of the ambulance district back home. He had another year, and he'd be retiring. I'd hoped they would join us on an RV adventure, but Lizbeth had put her foot down. She babysat her four grandchildren, and nothing short of all her kids moving out of state would convince her to go on a road trip. Lizbeth and Donny had deeply planted roots in Missouri. Mo and I didn't have to worry. Both our girls lived out of state. Carrie was married to Michael and had Ben, our only grandchild. Sadie was still single, but recently Carrie had confided in me that she thought Sadie was seeing someone.

"Excellent idea." Mo set the knife down. A little too firmly, if you ask me.

We finished eating while Max stared us down.

"I almost forgot to tell you; the guy next door came over while I was getting the grill ready. Turns out he's a fisherman. He rented a boat and invited me to fish tomorrow."

I knew this would happen. Our vacation had turned into a "his" vacation and a "her" vacation. If I had to look forward to a summer filled with occupying my time, I'd better find a hobby to keep me busy. Good thing I'd loaded my e-reader with several cozy mysteries before we left. "My day is already planned. I'm doing yoga in the morning, and then I'll find a shady spot at the pool to read. Max and I will have a quiet, laid-back day while you swap fish tales with a stranger and drink beer. Don't worry about me," I said sarcastically.

Mo laughed. "Not much beer drinking since we're going at six in the morning. We'll be back long before beer drinking time. But I reserve the right to invite him and his wife over for a beer tomorrow night."

"And I still reserve the right to dislike this place," I said.

"Huh?"

I tapped my fitness tracker. "I have twenty-four hours, right? If this place doesn't grow on me, we're out of here at four thirty tomorrow."

"Whatever you say, boss lady. Now, what's for dessert? I had my mind set on pie, but you foiled that."

"There's still pie on the driveway. I can get you a fork." I stuck out my tongue. "Otherwise, it's fresh strawberries and pound cake—homemade."

Mo eyed the pie. "I think I'll have strawberries and pound cake."

"Smart man." I rose from the table.

Olive and another woman zipped into the driveway in a golf cart. Olive hopped out, glancing at the pie, then motioned for the other woman to join her.

Max scrambled to his feet, let out a warning growl, and positioned himself between Mo and me. Mo reached down and rubbed his head. "Shh, it's okay."

Max eyed the women warily. They strode over to the picnic table where Mo sat eagerly awaiting his dessert.

"How's it going, folks?" Olive asked.

"Good," Mo said. "Mattie here's getting ready to bring out some pound cake for dessert if you'd like to join us."

Olive waved him off. "No, thanks."

"You sure? I was just heading inside to dish it up," I said.

Max, satisfied we weren't going to be kidnapped, curled up on his bed, keeping an eye on the ladies.

"We're good," Olive said, "but I wanted to introduce you to Kat and check to see if you were settling in okay. She's got her RV the next street over, and she has a booth at the flea market. Kat, this is Mattie and Mo Modesky. They just pulled in today."

The woman looked like she'd stepped out of the seventies. She wore a brightly colored paisley broomstick skirt, topped with a white peasant blouse and a suede-fringed vest. Her more-salt-than-pepper hair had been twisted into a single waist-length braid. If she added a pair of granny glasses, she'd be set.

"Hi," Mo and I said in unison.

"Hey back," she said.

"At least stay for a beer," Mo said.

Olive looked at Kat. "What do you think?"

"Just one, because I need to go back to my booth."

"Is the flea market still open?" I asked.

She sat down. "No, I left my wallet."

I went in and grabbed four beers. When I came back, Mo was bent over his tackle box examining fishing lures.

I slid two beers to Kat and Olive. "I'm sorry. I would have invited you inside if I'd known he was going to abandon you."

They shrugged and twisted off the caps on their beers.

Olive laughed. "Fishing tackle takes more precedent in these parts anyway. Man's gotta make sure his gear is in order."

Kat chuckled and clinked her bottle against Olive's. "Truth."

Mo retrieved a beer and went back to the tackle box. I cut him a warning glance. He shrugged.

"Do you come here often?" I asked Kat, sounding like I'd just slung a pick-up line at the local bar.

"All the time," she replied. "I supplement my pension selling at flea markets."

"What do you sell?"

"Leather goods."

"Oh, I bet that's the booth where I saw the cute purse. I'm going back tomorrow to look at it. My best friend has a birthday coming up."

"Hard to say," she said. "There are a couple of booths similar to mine."

"You get any grief from the other owners for selling similar products?" I thought about Cal and Sandi's argument and wondered how many others dealt with the same situations.

"Not from the other leather sellers," she said.

"From someone else?" I wondered if Cal was harassing her too. I couldn't vent to Mo about what it felt like to watch some floozy ogling my husband, and I still didn't like the idea of making nice with Cal. I wouldn't mind sharing a common enemy with Kat.

Olive frowned. "Why? What have you heard?"

"I overheard an argument between two booth owners today that got pretty heated."

"That's a regular occurrence," Kat said.

"It's nothing to concern yourself with," Olive said.

Her flat tone suggested she wasn't one to gossip and didn't appreciate hearing it from others. I frowned and changed the subject. "We're from Pine Grove. How about you?" I asked Kat.

"Sedalia."

"That's where the state fair is, right?"

"Yes." She twisted her watch around and stared at it. "Olive, are we about done? I need to get my wallet."

"Sure thing." Olive set her bottle on the table. "Thanks for the beer. Guess we better get going. I need to close the gates to the flea market before I head home." Olive coughed several times, pulled a tissue from her pocket, and dabbed at her nose. "Sorry, allergies." She continued to cough. "Could I trouble you for some water?" She coughed again.

"Sure thing. Be right back." I ran inside and grabbed a bottle of water from the fridge.

When I returned, her coughs had subsided, but her eyes still watered.

"Thank you." She took a long drink of water. "I'm not sure what's in bloom, but it's driving me nuts."

"Glad I could help. I brought a couple of cough drops, too, if you want them." I placed them on the table.

"Thanks." She unwrapped one and popped it in her mouth. "We better go. If you need anything, call." She pulled a business card from her pocket and handed it to me.

CHAPTER THREE

I'd waited almost too long to get in a lengthy walk with Max, but I knew if we didn't, he'd have me up in the middle of the night for a pitstop. I'd rather go out now than at 2:00 a.m. Plus, Mo had been on me again to buddy up to Cal. That did not go over well. I needed the walk as much for me as I did for Max.

When I finally leashed him and set out, the sun had set, and streetlights flickered on. We passed the neighboring RV. Shadows from their TV played across the window. We turned onto the main road.

"Kind of vacant around, huh, Max?"

A figure clad in black ran toward me, light reflecting off the toes of the runner's shoes. I took a deep breath. As the runner approached, Max wagged his tail. He hadn't given a warning growl, so I relaxed.

"Miss Mattie, why are you out so late?" Sarge stopped in front of me, stooped down to tighten his laces, and scratched Max behind the ear.

"I guess I needed some fresh air." My voice sounded as disgusted as I felt.

"Oh, did the knife not go over so well?"

"No, it was fine. I'm just in a mood." I lightened my tone, trying to put Cal out of my mind. "What brings you out this late?"

"A run at night is the perfect ending to my day. I run first thing in the morning before the sun comes up and last thing at night before I go to bed. The air is cool, traffic is light, and there's no one around. I better get going." Sarge gave Max one last scratch and jogged off, calling over his shoulder, "You be careful out here by yourself."

Max and I watched until Sarge disappeared into the darkness, me marveling at the sweet scent of jasmine in the air and Max snapping at fireflies that dared cross his path. A train whistle sounded in the distance followed by the occasional yap of a nearby dog. Max paid the sounds no attention. We continued walking toward the office. My thoughts returned to Cal, and my anger reignited. Not so much at Mo but at myself for letting her get to me. Make friends, my hiney. What I wanted to do was give the woman a piece of my mind.

Max pulled me toward a tree. I stopped while he did his business, and I thought of all the things I should have said to Cal. What really burned my biscuit was that I had thought of all the good stuff to hit her with after she'd left. The more I thought about it, the more I fumed.

"You about done?" I pulled a treat from my pocket. "Let's find Cal's place and get this over with." I had no intention of letting my words go to waste. I needed to say them, and she needed to hear them. Mo was too nice to tell her to back off. Besides, I think he may have enjoyed the attention and seeing me riled up.

I took stock of my location and realized I needed to turn around. Cal had told Mo she lived on a corner lot on the third street, one street past ours in the permanent resident section

Sarge had told me about. The units looked stationary—no wheels. She'd said her place had Chinese lanterns hanging on the porch. As we walked, I counted the streets until I stood outside Cal's home, staring at her gaudy lanterns. The glow created eerie spectacles swaying in the wind.

Max cocked his head.

"What's the matter?" I tugged on his leash, but he refused to move. "You don't like her either."

He growled a low growl that made the hair on my arms rise.

I took a step forward. Max came around in front of me and growled again—a low, almost imperceptible growl, a growl to warn me but not one to alert anyone else.

I bent down and ran my hand along his back, smoothing his hackles. "Shh! Let's turn around and go home. It's okay," I whispered, more to myself than to him. I hadn't expected him to dislike her that much, but I shouldn't have been surprised. I'd have it out with Cal tomorrow.

A person dressed in black came around from the back of Cal's place. At first, I thought it was Sarge and started to wave, but when they saw me, they zigzagged, made an abrupt turn, and headed down the main road in the direction I'd just come from. Max growled then jerked on the leash. I lost my grip, and off he went in a flurry of barking and snarling.

"Max! Come back!" I stood in the street, not knowing what to do. My heart pounded as panic threatened to overwhelm me.

Why? Why had he run off? That wasn't like him at all. He hadn't run after Sarge earlier. "Max!" I yelled, shaking a small bag of treats, hoping to get his attention. For an old dog, he could flat-out run when he wanted to.

I ran after him until the throbbing in my left knee forced me to slow down. Between rubbing my knee and catching my breath, I continued calling Max, hoping he'd come back. I was torn between going back to the RV and getting Mo or continuing to chase after Max.

Getting Mo would take too long. I dug into my pocket for my phone and came up empty-handed. That left me no choice. I wasn't in any shape to chase him and hoped he'd found an insomniac squirrel rather than trouble. It sure looked like he'd gone after that stranger. Scary thoughts crept into my mind and drew a chill up my spine, but I knew better than to let them linger.

I convinced myself to go back to the RV and get Mo. I'd had more than enough surprises in my lifetime to go off chasing the prospect of another.

As I walked back to the RV, I continued calling for Max. The Jeep Wrangler we'd towed behind the RV was not in the driveway where Mo had parked it.

"What the heck?" Where would Mo go this late? It was after nine. I found my phone, which I'd left on the table, and saw I'd missed several text messages.

MO: FORGOT TO GET A FISHING LICENSE WHEN WE WERE AT THE STORE. BE BACK SOON.

MO: TURNS OUT OLD GUYS DON'T NEED ONE. RAN INTO AN OLD BUDDY FROM THE POLICE ACADEMY, GOING FOR A BEER.

MO: DON'T WAIT UP.

My anger ratcheted several notches. I jabbed the screen.

ME: MAX RAN AWAY!!!!

Nothing.

I gave him another minute then punched in his cell number.

"What?" he answered.

"What? I sent you a text that Max got loose and ran away." I heard country music in the background and a woman's voice. "Where are you, and who are you with?" Immediately an image of Cal popped up in my head. He wouldn't. He better not.

"What? I can't hear you. Just a minute." The background sounds died away. "Is that better?"

"Where are you?" I shouted, louder than I needed to, but loud enough to get my point across.

There was silence. Then, in a quiet voice, Mo said, "I'm at a little bar in town having a beer with a buddy from the academy. Didn't you get my text?"

"A male buddy?" I asked, ignoring his question.

He sighed. "Of course."

Female laughter erupted.

"Oh, that," Mo said. "There's some kind of bachelorette party going on here. What's going on with Max? What happened?"

Tears stung my eyes. "When I wasn't paying attention, he pulled the leash right out of my hand and took off."

"That doesn't sound like him. That dog is practically attached to you."

I explained to Mo about the figure I'd seen by Cal's place. "Max growled then off he went. I walked everywhere, looking for him. When he didn't come, I didn't know what else to do, so here I am. He's not familiar with this place like he is home. I'm really worried. Do you think he can find his way back?"

"You saw someone sneaking around the RV park?" Mo asked, ignoring my concern.

I scoffed. "Not really sneaking. Sarge, the guy from the flea market, was out for an evening run earlier. The guy's gotta be eighty or something. Maybe he wore himself out and took a shortcut back home. I passed him once, but then I turned around and started back. I guess it's feasible he turned around, too, and was heading back to his place. He lives over in that area somewhere. But I have to admit, it kind of creeped me out. Max didn't growl the first time he passed us. But this time he growled and snarled and then ran off."

"When I get back, I'll go looking for him. He'll probably beat me there."

I huffed out a breath. "He's not even familiar with the area. Who knows if he can even find his way back?"

"He's got street smarts. Don't worry. Go on to bed. I'll be home soon."

"I'm not going to bed until I know he's safe," I said.

"Suit yourself. I'd tell you not to wait up, but that probably won't fly either."

"You aren't coming home now?" My voice rose an octave, and I sounded shriller than I had intended. But I needed to make a point since my husband was not one to take a hint.

"In a bit. We ordered another round right before you called."

I hit the disconnect button. Max could be lying dead in a ditch for all Mo cared. I went outside and hollered for Max until the lights in the next RV came on. My knee ached, and I knew I couldn't go roaming around. If I screwed my knee up, I'd be headed for surgery. I glanced at the fairy lights, hoping they would help Max find us, then went inside and took two pain relievers, put an ice pack on my knee, and lay on the couch. I wanted to stay close to the door in case he came back.

I must have dozed off, because when I woke up, Mo was kneeling next to me.

"Hey," he said. "I walked over the entire park looking for him."

Rubbing the sleep out of my eyes, I sat up. "What time is it?"

"A little after eleven. I took a raincheck on the beer then came back to get a flashlight. You were out cold, so I let you sleep and went out looking." He rubbed my knee. "Noticed the ice pack. What happened?"

"Nothing, just acting up like it always does." I guess I couldn't be mad. He'd left a perfectly good beer to come and look for Max. "I'm so worried about him."

"He'll be okay. I put his food and water outside by the door. If he's not back by morning, I'll call my buddy at the sheriff's department and ask them to keep an eye out. If you make up some flyers on that laptop of yours, I'll post them around after I get back from fishing." Mo tugged my hand. "Come on. Let's go to bed."

CHAPTER FOUR

Mo left before sunrise to meet his new fishing buddy. After making up a flyer, I tucked the flash drive in my pocket, hoping Olive would let me print them at the office. Max's food bowl and water remained untouched. I freshened the water and headed to the rec center. The office didn't open for another hour, but I knew Olive would be at yoga.

Four women were milling around the room when I walked in. I recognized Olive and Kat. The third favored Cal, except with short, spiky platinum hair instead of red. I'd not met the fourth.

Olive waved. "Come on in and let me introduce you. We're waiting on Cal. Then we'll get started."

"I have a favor to ask, if you don't mind." I explained about Max while the other women watched. "Would you mind terribly if Mo went around handing out or hanging flyers until we find Max?"

She patted my hand. "Of course not. You can even put one up in the office if you think it'll help."

I held up the flash drive. "I don't have a way to print them off and wondered—"

She snatched it out of my hand. "Don't you worry about a

thing. I'll print as many as you need after class. Then I'll bring them down to you when I open up the gates to the flea market. Now let me introduce you. We'll get you relaxed with a little yoga."

"I need to get back," I said.

"Nonsense. You need to focus and center. Yoga is just the thing for that." Olive rounded up the women. "Everyone, this is Mattie. She and her husband, Mo, checked in yesterday. And their dog went missing. So, keep an eye out. He's a handsome black lab." Olive moved over next to the platinum-haired woman. "Mattie, this is Ruby, Cal's sister."

"You can't just introduce me as Ruby? Why do you always have to attach Cal's name? I'm Ruby Wallace. Just Ruby. See how easily that glides off the tongue. When you introduce Cal to people, do you introduce her as Ruby's sister?" Ruby pulled a bottle of water out of her bag and twisted off the cap.

Olive curled her lip. "Mattie, that's Ruby. Just Ruby." She nodded to the other woman. "This is Sandi."

"Sandi with an *I*," said a tanned woman around my age. Cottony hair, tinted a curious shade of pink, surrounded her face like a helmet. She winked and let out a howling laugh I instantly fell in love with.

I recognized her melodic voice. She was the woman I'd overheard arguing with Cal at the flea market.

"She's Kat," the woman named Sandi said, hooking her thumb at Kat. "Don't ask her what Kat stands for. That's apparently a secret."

"We've met." Kat wore her salt-and-pepper braid twisted and pinned to her head like a crown. She'd replaced the paisley skirt with orange leggings covered in bright pink and yellow daisies and a yellow tank top covered with an over-sized white button-down shirt. "Olive and I stopped by last night."

"Nice to meet everyone." Yoga mats lay on the floor in front of each woman. "Do I need one of those?"

"Unless you want to do yoga on the bare floor." Ruby snickered. "Have you never done yoga before?"

Sandi nudged me. "I didn't have one when I first started either. Cal has a stack of extras if you need one." She pointed to a pile of exercise equipment near the door.

"Speaking of Cal," Olive said, "where is she?"

We all turned to Ruby.

"What? I'm not her keeper. Jeez, would you cut me a break? I'm her sister, but I'm not attached to her hip."

Sandi leaned in and whispered, "Sounds like someone is a wee bit cranky this morning."

Ruby sneered. "I heard that. Are we going to do yoga or stand around and blabber all day? I've got a booth to open before the customers show up."

"Yeah, I need to get mine open," Kat said.

"Ruby, will you do the honors since Cal's not here?" Olive asked.

Ruby stomped to the front of the room and switched on an ancient boom box. The soothing sounds of flute music filled the room.

"You ever do yoga before?" Olive asked me.

I nodded. "I took a free class back home. It was a sample to see if the center could draw enough support to have it. Apparently six baby boomers in spandex didn't make the grade, because the center dropped the idea and added Zumba instead. One class was all I lasted. I tripped over my feet, screwed up my knee, and had to quit."

Sandi and Olive laughed. Ruby glared. Kat was already getting into a yoga pose and paid me no attention.

I grabbed a mat and found a spot next to Sandi.

"Deep breaths," Ruby said.

I watched Sandi and mimicked what she did.

After several seconds, Ruby said, "Mountain pose."

"Maybe this wasn't the best idea I've ever had." I didn't have a clue what a mountain pose was.

Sandi laughed. "Just watch me if it's unfamiliar."

Ruby cleared her throat. "You're breaking the silence."

"Pardon me all to heck." Sandi rolled her eyes. "She's all full of herself today."

"I'm done. If you won't take this seriously, then I will not stand here and listen to you make a mockery out of yoga." Ruby rolled up her mat and tucked it under her arm. "I've got better things to do."

"Oh, don't be such a poop," Olive said. "Lighten up. Not everything has to be so solemn."

Several other women entered the room as Ruby stalked out.

"Yoga's over for the day," Olive said to the newcomers. "Come back Monday, and we'll give it another try."

A chorus of grumbles and groans followed.

"We don't have yoga tomorrow since it's Sunday," Sandi said to me. "Shall we head home? You're parked next to us. I saw you when you were setting up."

"Oh, well, hello neighbor. Mo said he was going fishing with a neighbor. Was that your husband?"

"It was. Stan and I stopped by last night to introduce ourselves. Your husband said you were out walking the dog. We had a beer and a pleasant chat. Your hubby seems like a nice guy. He and Stan hit it off. Stan lives on the water. You'll be lucky to see your man all week.

"Stan is addicted to fishing, but there'll be good eats every night for dinner." Sandi rolled her mat and I followed, dropping the one I'd used back onto the stack.

The conversation never stopped as we walked home. It was like we'd known one another for ages instead of thirty minutes.

When we got to our street, I said, "I'm going to go check on Cal. I need to talk to her anyway." I couldn't do anything about Max until Olive brought me the flyers, but I still wanted to have a chat with Cal about keeping her distance from my husband. Checking on her would be a good excuse.

"It's not like her to miss yoga. She's a fanatic about it."

I explained about the person I'd seen running from Cal's place last night on my walk with Max. I hadn't thought much of it since then, but now that Sandi mentioned missing yoga, I felt a certain urgency that troubled me.

"That's odd. Mind if I tag along?" Sandi bent down to tie her shoe.

Who tagged along when something suspicious was afoot? Ugh. Why had I told her? I could hardly speak my mind with Sandi there. "Sure."

Sandi straightened. "She and I had it out yesterday."

"I heard. She raised quite a ruckus." We continued past our street and headed to the residential section.

Sandi's eyes rounded. "Gossip travels quickly."

"Not gossip. I was in the booth next to yours when she had her hissy fit," I said.

"She gets so worked up. I've been selling the same jewelry in my booth forever. It isn't even close to what she sells." Sandi wiggled her wrist and displayed a gorgeous bracelet with pale green pieces of sea glass set in silver. "Everything I sell, I make myself—earrings, necklaces, bracelets. Stan does all the metalwork. Cal sells stuff she buys from a catalog and marks up. Nothing unique about it."

"Your bracelet is lovely. I'll definitely have to stop by. My friend Lizbeth would absolutely love that. She's such a jewelry diva. I buy stuff for myself all the time but rarely wear it. I can't seem to get the right look going."

"Come by, and I'll help you. I have a great selection this year," Sandi said.

We stopped at Cal's driveway.

"Let me run up and check on her. I'll be right back." I jogged up the driveway, hoping my knee wouldn't give out. Taking Max for a walk yesterday didn't really count as exercise. My heart rate never increased because he was too busy stopping and sniffing to keep up any kind of pace.

The door to the living room was open, allowing me a full view of the inside. Only a metal screen door separated me from the room. I tapped on the frame and waited. "Anybody home?"

A little dachshund skittered across the floor, yapping like he weighed seventy pounds and would tear me to bits.

"Hey, little guy, is your mama home?"

The pup answered my question with a series of furious barks.

"Cal, it's Mattie Modesky. I met you at the office yesterday. Hello?" I pressed my face against the screen.

The dog raced across the room and out of sight, still barking.

"What's taking so long?"

I startled and screamed.

"Holy crap, did I scare you?" Sandi stood right beside me.

I gulped and laughed. "Ha! Yeah, don't know why I'm so jumpy."

The little dog came roaring back full tilt, barking.

"Hey, Scooter," Sandi said.

The dog looked up at Sandi and whined.

"I guess she's not here. Maybe she's at the flea market already," I said. "I'll catch up with her later."

"No," Sandi said. "This is bizarre. She would never leave Scooter alone while she's at her booth. He's always with her."

"Could be around back."

Sandi ignored me and pulled open the screen door. "I'm going in. She might have fallen in the shower. She may be spry, but she's still almost eighty."

I touched her arm. "Let's go get help."

"Cal and I have had our problems, but people around here watch out for one another. Most everyone here is a senior citizen. We get people slipping and falling all the time." Sandi reached down and patted the dog who jumped and barked like the devil possessed him. "Last year when Stan and I were here, old Mr. Gaber four units over had a stroke. Didn't show up for poker night. If the guys hadn't checked on him, the docs say he wouldn't have made it. They took him to the hospital in a helicopter. Now he's zippy as ever and still playing poker."

Despite my uneasiness, I followed her down the narrow hallway.

Cal lay on the bed, sheets rumpled all around her. Scooter dashed up a little ramp attached to the side of the bed and licked Cal's face. She didn't budge.

"Cal!" Sandi hollered. "Wake up."

I stopped and backed up. An icy tingle ran up my spine. Cal's coloring didn't look good. "Sandi, we need to leave and call for help."

"Don't be silly. The crazy old bat probably took a sleeping pill." Sandi wiggled Cal's toe. When the woman didn't move, Sandi walked up to the side of the bed. She stood there for a moment as if someone had pressed pause on the TV, then let out a bloodcurdling scream.

"What?" Tiny hairs on the nape of my neck prickled. I inched closer and saw why Sandi screamed.

A knife stuck out of Cal's neck, and she lay drenched in a pool of blood. I wanted to look away, to run away, but the knife caught my attention. The bone handle had the same eagle as the one I purchased for Mo. The "no two are alike—guaranteed" pocketknife.

CHAPTER FIVE

Sandi and I sat on a picnic table while paramedics and a deputy attended to Cal. Sandi had leashed Scooter and brought him outside. He sat at our feet, trembling and whining.

I pulled a treat from the stash in my pocket and gave him one, hoping to quiet him. He sniffed but refused it.

"This cannot be happening," Sandi said. Her entire body trembled.

I was still trying to wrap my mind around the total scene and making mental notes on what I'd seen. Sandi had vomited, which would drive the crime scene investigators nuts. I had pulled myself together and glanced around the room, checking for anything that might be out of place or odd. Not that I'd know what that was since I'd never been inside Cal's before.

"That knife," Sandi said. "It was one like Sarge sells in his booth. I bought Stan one last year with a heron carved on it. I'd know them anywhere."

"Are they really one of a kind?" The image of that knife was emblazoned in my mind. I wanted nothing more than to get home and check Mo's knife. Maybe the eagle faced a different direction or maybe the wings fanned out differently, but Mo was out on the boat with Sandi's husband. I'd have to wait until they came home. Who knew when that would be?

Sandi narrowed her eyes. "Why aren't you more shook up? You act like this is an everyday occurrence."

I didn't want to lie to her, but I didn't dare tell her about what I'd been through at Christmas when Lizbeth and I found a dead elf stuffed into a charity donation box. Not that he was a real elf. He'd just dressed up in an elf costume.

"My husband is a retired police chief. You wouldn't believe the stuff I've seen and heard." Mission accomplished. No lie there. "A dead body can't hurt you. What bothers me more is that it happened. I was skeptical when we arrived yesterday. Why do you and your husband keep coming back? Surely, there are nicer places to stay."

"I guess. We've always felt safe. Heck, we never even lock our doors. We will now. We've been coming here so long, I guess we've grown immune. It used to be so nice, and we just never realized it was getting run-down. Since Olive's husband died, this is her only income, and we'd rather put the money in her pocket than some conglomerate that owns RV parks all over the country."

"You're not worried now?" I asked. "About safety?"

Sandi shook her head. "Nah! Cal irked a lot of people. This wasn't random. You aren't worried, are you?"

A deputy wearing mirrored sunglasses ambled toward us.

"Don't look now, but I think the interrogation is about to begin," I said, dodging her question.

"That's Deputy Beau," Sandi said.

"You know him?"

"Yeah, he's a pain in the butt. He's always out here for one thing or another," Sandi said.

"Jeez, I thought you said it was safe. If we'd known it was crime-ridden, we'd have gone somewhere else." I made a mental note to double-check the next place where we had reservations. The last thing I wanted was to be in the middle of another murder investigation.

"Not for criminal stuff. For old people stuff. You know strokes, heart attacks, falls. Every time an ambulance comes, they dispatch a deputy too. Beau almost always gets the call."

"Good morning, ladies," Deputy Beau said as he approached.

"What's so good about it?" Sandi said.

"You make a fair point." The deputy took a seat across from us.

People from the neighboring units gathered in the street.

"Nothing to see here, folks. Go on back in and eat your breakfast." Deputy Beau made a shooing motion with his hands.

When they didn't disperse, he stood up. "Don't make me get out my citation book. Now go on. Go home. Let us do our job. I'm sure these ladies will spread the gossip soon enough." He hiked an eyebrow and glared at Sandi. "Right?"

Sandi wrinkled her nose.

The neighbors went back to their business, dragging their feet as they went.

Deputy Beau sat back down. "Now which one of you ladies found Cal? And what were the circumstances that led you to enter the premises?"

"We both did," I said.

"And you are?" He pulled a notebook from his pocket and made an entry.

"Mattie Modesky. Mattie with two *T*s."

He looked up; his eyebrows had scrunched together.

"Not Maddie with two *D*s. It's pronounced differently, but people rarely catch the *T* sound and assume it's a *D* sound." Why was I jabbering like a mynah bird?

"Right. And she's Sandi with an *I*." He shook his head. "I remember. What I don't remember is your last name, Sandi."

"Clayton," she said through chattering teeth. "Sandi Clayton."

"Which brings us to why you were here in the first place."

"Cal didn't show up for yoga this morning," I said.

"And?" the deputy prodded.

"And we came to check on her," I said.

"You didn't think maybe she'd overslept? Instead, you felt it necessary to traipse over here and let yourselves in."

Sandi nodded.

"That would pretty much be it," I said. I didn't know why I left out the part about the person I'd seen last night, but it seemed like the thing to do. It wasn't like I'd seen the person come out of her place. If it was Sarge cutting through, I didn't want to set off an alarm that would make him look like a suspect.

"The door was open. Cal wouldn't go to bed with only the screen door closed. Scooter here was going nuts." Sandi picked up the little dog and hugged it close to her. "Right, baby. You knew something wasn't right, didn't you?"

Scooter nuzzled into her neck.

"Give me the rundown from the time you woke until right now," Deputy Beau said. "You first." He pointed his pen at Sandi.

Sandi recited her complete schedule, starting when she'd rolled out of bed, including the fact that she'd eaten a handful of prunes and drunk a glass of orange-flavored fiber drink. "If I take off running, I hope you understand." She grinned.

I recited my morning, leaving out the fact that Mo had gotten a little frisky before leaving for his fishing trip. I never managed to stay mad at him long. What happened in the RV was no one's business but mine and Mo's.

"Any reason you can think of why someone would have it in for Cal?" the deputy asked.

Sandi smirked. "Beyond the obvious. Every married

woman in the RV park. Ha! Probably every married woman in the county."

The deputy pointed his pen at Sandi. "She ever come on to your husband?"

"Every opportunity she got. I ignored her. Stan's pilot light went out a long time ago."

That was definitely more information than I wanted to know. But it also made me wonder if Stan's pilot light had been ignited elsewhere.

"Any other reasons you can think of?" the deputy asked.

"Nope," Sandi said.

I noticed she hadn't mentioned her ongoing feud over the jewelry booth.

"How about you?" He turned his attention to me.

"I only met the woman once," I said. Twice if you counted when she brought Mo the pie.

"Yet, you felt compelled to check on her when she didn't show up at a yoga class?"

"I met her in the office when we checked in yesterday afternoon," I said.

Beau looked over the top of his sunglasses. "And?"

Dang, he was good. I figured I might as well tell him about my run-in with Cal. He'd hear about it anyway once he talked to Olive. And he would talk to Olive, of that I was certain. And Sarge and every other husband and wife in the RV park.

"Yes, she came on to my husband. So what? She's seventy-something years old." I preened a bit. My sixty-fifth birthday was rapidly approaching. With a few extra pounds and a slight pooch to my stomach, I wasn't a beauty queen by any stretch of the imagination, but I still knew how to keep my man at home.

The deputy coughed and covered his mouth with his hand, but I saw the grin he failed to suppress. "Tell me everything you touched once you got here."

I looked at Sandi, and she looked at me.

"Did I open the door?" Sandi asked.

I nodded.

He wrote that in his notebook. "Once you were inside?"

"Nothing," I said. "At least, I don't think I did."

Sandi shivered. "I touched Cal's toe."

Deputy Beau's head snapped up. "You what?"

"I mean not actually her toe," Sandi backtracked. "Her foot was under the sheet. I thought she was sleeping, so I wiggled her toe through the sheet to wake her up."

"Oh." The deputy made another entry.

"I think that's it," Sandi said.

"Who tossed their cookies?" the deputy asked.

I pointed to Sandi. "That would be her."

Sandi nodded. "Sorry."

"Did either of you touch the knife?"

Sandi shook her head. "O-M-G no. Absolutely not."

"What about you?"

"No, my husband is a retired police chief. I know better." I enjoyed sharing my knowledge about police stuff. Mo was an outstanding police officer, and I was proud of his service to our little community back home. At least I hadn't touched *that* knife. Unless it was Mo's knife. If that was the case, my prints would be all over it. And Mo's would too. My smugness evaporated.

Deputy Beau smirked. "That doesn't cut the bait with me, lady. You're new around here, aren't you?"

I nodded.

"One of you had to open the door to leave. Which one of you opened it?"

Sandi and I shared another glance and both shrugged at the same time.

"Looks like I'll be fingerprinting both of you." He pulled two business cards from his pocket and handed them to us.

"Come down to the station this afternoon and get printed. Ask for Lou Ann."

A golf cart pulled up and stopped in the street. Ruby jumped out. "What the devil is going on here?"

Deputy Beau lumbered over to the golf cart, talking as he went. "Miss Ruby, I'm afraid I have some awful . . ." His voice trailed off as he got out of normal voice range.

Ruby eyed Scooter snuggling in Sandi's arms and dropped to her knees. "No! No! No!" she screamed.

Sandi gouged me in the ribs, rolled her eyes at Ruby's carrying on, and whispered, "You thinking what I'm thinking?"

"I don't guess so. What are you thinking?"

"I'm thinking Cal's death might have something to do with Ruby's pissy mood this morning," Sandi said.

My mouth dropped open. "You mean Ruby already knew Cal was dead when we were at yoga?" Was she accusing Ruby of Cal's murder or of covering up Cal's murder?

Sandi hiked her lip. "It's not like she came and checked on Cal when Cal didn't show up."

"She's her sister. That would be pretty cold. Don't they live together?" I asked.

"Heavens, no. Ruby lives two streets over. They shared an RV when they first started coming here, but when they became permanent residents, they each rented their own place. They both have an affinity for men and, well . . . that doesn't work out when you have a roommate, if you know what I mean."

"They're almost eighty. I can't even imagine chasing a man at that age." I stared at Ruby, who had snuggled into Deputy Beau's arms and was bawling like a baby. She ran a hand up and down his muscled back. "Tell me it's my imagination, but isn't she playing that up a bit?"

Sandi waved her hand. "Oh honey, you haven't seen Ruby at work, have you? I hate to speak ill of the dead, but between

Cal and Ruby, it's always open season on men. It's a toss-up who's the biggest flirt."

"I thought Olive told me that Cal and Sarge were an item," I said.

"In Cal's dreams. You've seen Sarge. For an old guy, he's a catch. Rumor has it he has a lady friend. He takes Cal out to Catfish Haven for their buy-one-get-one-free dinner once a week, but that's the extent of it." She eyed Ruby, who was still fondling the deputy. "Any man will do for Ruby. Not that Deputy Hunk over there isn't well worth a good squeeze, but puh-leeze, he's what, thirty-five tops. She has underwear older than him."

I busted out a chuckle then checked myself. No telling who was watching. I didn't want to appear insensitive. "You remind me a lot of my friend back home. You have the same sense of humor."

"Glad I could inject some levity, considering the circumstances. I wonder how long we have to stay. Is it in poor taste to say I really need to get my booth open?"

"You could tell him the prunes were getting down to business," I said.

She shook her head. "Sadly, they aren't. It'll probably happen about the time I open my booth." Her mouth dropped open. "Do you think they'll let the flea market open today? Olive will have a fit if they make her close. She'll have to refund all our booth rents, and that'll make her mad."

"I don't see why," I said.

"Did that sound crude? I didn't mean it to. It's just, we're only here another week, and I always make good money. Keeps Stan off my back about how much I spend at the craft store."

A female deputy arrived, and Deputy Beau tore himself from Ruby's grip and handed her off.

"Smart thinking on his part," Sandi said. "Ruby's like a tick. She sticks to the first man who comes along."

"I heard that," the deputy said, heading our way. "She's had an awful shock."

"Sorry, I didn't mean it that way," Sandi said.

I stood up. "How much longer do you need us?"

"Yeah," Sandi said, picking up on my hint. "I may need to find a bathroom."

"Go on. Just remember to come down to the station for those prints," the deputy said.

"I'll go as soon as the flea market closes for the evening." Sandi hopped off the table and put Scooter on the ground.

"What are you going to do with him?" I asked.

"I don't know." Sandi looked down at the dachshund. "What do you think, little guy?"

He wove between Sandi's ankles, tangling her in the leash.

"Stan will kill me."

"Don't look at me," I said. "Max is eating us out of—" Tears pricked my eyes. "I need to get back and see if Olive dropped off those flyers."

"I don't suppose you'd take Scooter until—"

I cut her off. "Absolutely not."

"Sorry. That was lame of me," Sandi said.

"What about Ruby?"

"No way. She hates Scooter. I'll take my chances with Stan until I can figure out what to do."

CHAPTER SIX

"Hey, Miss Mattie." Sarge waved a greeting from behind the table in his booth.

I waved back. "Good morning."

Sandi and I had parted ways at the corner of our street. She wanted to get Scooter settled so she could come back and open her booth. Olive had left the flyers and my flash drive in an envelope under a rock on the picnic table.

My mind was still reeling after seeing a knife identical to Mo's sticking out of Cal. A feeling of dread settled in the pit of my stomach. I knew Mo had nothing to do with Cal's death, but I also knew how police investigations worked; Mo had no alibi from the time he left the bar until the time he woke me up. If someone had seen him when he was out looking for Max, that would only raise suspicions higher.

I grabbed the flyers and headed to the flea market to see if I could post one at each booth and talk to Sarge about the uniqueness of his knives. Mo's knife was safe and sound in his pocket out on the lake. An identical knife had to be a coincidence. There had to be an explanation, and the only person who could help was Sarge. If Sandi's description of Ruby was correct, once the police finished with her and she got her act together, she'd be down at the flea market hanging onto Sarge. What better way to get a man's attention than by seeking sympathy?

I was so bad; I should have slapped myself for that thought. It wasn't like I knew any of these people well enough to make a judgment—not even Sandi. My focus was Sarge. I didn't want him distracted when I asked him about the knife.

By the time I arrived at his booth, my flyers hung in several others. Each owner had assured me they'd keep an eye out for Max. I wanted to get as many eyes as possible on that flyer.

"What brings you back?" Sarge asked as I approached his table.

I could see why Cal chased after him like a groupie. His trim physique, probably from his daily run, shaved years off his age. Silver hair, cut military-style, finished off the look. Today he wore casual but expensive-looking golf attire.

I handed him a flyer and explained about Max, asking if he'd give the flyer a prominent location in his booth.

"Sure thing." He tore a piece of tape from a dispenser on the table and placed a flyer front and center on a display rack. "How does that look?"

I made a circle out of my thumb and forefinger. "A-OK. Thank you."

"Sorry about your dog. Hope you get him back."

"You didn't by any chance see him last night after we ran into you, did you?"

"No, I decided to cut my run early and head home," Sarge said.

Crap! So, maybe I did need to tell Deputy Beau about the person I'd seen. If it really wasn't Sarge, then he'd have nothing to worry about. Either way I'd be doing the right thing. And I didn't need to mention Sarge's name.

I lingered to look at the new items he'd put on display, not sure how to bring up the subject of the knife.

"Looks like you're eyeing the chef's knives. I have a nice selection of curved chopping knives too. Just unpacked them this morning." He took several from the display.

"Nope. I'm good. I have to stop looking. But they sure are nice." Buyer's remorse had always been a weakness I suffered. Lizbeth and I often joked about buying something one day and returning it the next. The other malady we shared was gift envy—buying a gift for the other and liking it so much we kept it and went back to buy another gift. We were so bad—as in every time we shopped for a gift—that we just started buying two at the outset.

"If you're not in the market for kitchen utensils, then what can I do for you?"

"Mo loved his knife. His best friend back home has a birthday in a couple of weeks, and I thought I'd see if you had another one like it. I think they'd get a kick out of having matching knives." I'd managed to get that out without telling a fib.

"No, ma'am. Each one is unique. The guy who makes them never repeats a design." Sarge pulled the case from a shelf and set it on the table. "See. Not a duplicate in the bunch."

"Would he do one for a special request? I'd sure love one for our friend. Maybe he could switch up the wings or have the eagle sitting instead of in flight. Is that a possibility?" I crossed my fingers for good measure.

Sarge shook his head. "I'm sorry, but it's part of his brand. Once he creates a design, he never does another one in any form." He selected one knife and held it out. "How about a falcon? This one's nice."

I frowned, hoping I looked disappointed enough to get him to reconsider and dig out another eagle knife. "No, I'm really set on an eagle."

"That's too bad. I wish I could help, but this guy is a stickler about not repeating his designs."

"Okay, I understand." My insides screamed. If what Sarge told me was true, the knife used to kill Cal did belong to Mo. How could that be? I thought about Cal's tiff with Sandi over selling jewelry. "Does anyone else sell a similar knife?"

Sarge puffed out his chest in a proud stance. "No, I've cornered the market. No one at the flea market can compete with the quality of the ones I sell, so they don't even try."

That was so not what I wanted to hear. How in the world did a knife like Mo's wind up in Cal's neck? I had a bad feeling I wouldn't like the answer.

I scrunched my lips together. "Good to know. At least Mo can enjoy his." Or not.

"What's the story with all the sirens?" Sarge asked, looking in the direction of the residential section of the RV park. "Somebody have a heart attack or stroke?"

"Oh, my goodness, haven't you heard?" *Why me? Why did I have to be the one to tell him? Why didn't I leave as soon as he dashed my hopes about the knife?*

"I haven't heard anything. Been too busy setting up. Saturdays are crazy. Around noon buses from neighboring communities arrive. Well, I hope they do. Unless we get more booths to fill this place, we could be doomed."

Was he the person I saw sneaking around Cal's place last night, or was it a coincidence? I saw Sarge when he was out running, then later saw someone who could have been him. *How do I tell him that Cal is dead? No, not just dead—murdered.*

I ran a quick strategy through my head, one that Mo used all the time when he worked on the police force. Tell as little as possible, leave out details, and watch for a reaction.

I focused on Sarge's face. "Something happened to Cal."

Nothing, not even a blink.

"What?" he asked.

"She didn't show up for yoga this morning." I took my time getting to the point, still monitoring his facial expression.

He scratched his chin. "Maybe she overslept."

"She didn't answer the door when Sandi and I went to check on her." Still dragging my feet. "So, we called 9-1-1."

"And?"

"And she's dead," I blurted out. Cop tactics wore me out. I got nothing from him. No facial response, nothing. Unless I didn't know what to look for. Did I miss a tic or an involuntary muscle twitch?

"Seriously?" He closed the case that held the knives and set it back on the shelf.

I nodded.

"Crap! That's bad. Was it her ticker? What am I asking? You wouldn't know that. Guess we'll have to wait and hear the details from Ruby." He glanced at his watch. "I'm sure she'll beat feet over here as soon as possible. She knows, doesn't she?"

I nodded again.

A golf cart raced up the aisle. I had a sneaking hunch it was Ruby coming to collect a hug and sympathy from Sarge.

～

"Can I interest you in a purse?" Kat pulled back the canvas booth flaps, tying them to metal posts that supported the top. "Oh, hey, Mattie."

I had visited every booth and left flyers. Kat's was the last. No one had seen Max. I'd put my phone number on the flyer, and my phone remained silent.

"Hi Kat." I handed her a flyer. "Olive dropped these off for me. Would you mind posting it? I'm hoping the more people who see it, the better."

She took the flyer and set it on the table. "Sure. What's going on in the park? I heard all kinds of sirens earlier."

Jeez, what was wrong with the rumor mill here? It had been at least two hours, and no one at the flea market had heard about Cal.

I repeated everything I'd told Sarge. I groaned inwardly when I realized I'd made the mistake of telling Kat about the person I'd seen running from Cal's. I'd not told Sarge, because that was about the time Ruby had roared up on her golf cart for a sympathetic hug. That and I didn't want him to think I was accusing him of something.

"That's creepy. Could you identify the person?" Kat asked.

"I don't know. It happened so quickly. I had seen Sarge earlier on our walk and just assumed it was him turning around and heading home. Now I'm not so sure. What if the person I saw was Cal's killer?"

Kat waved a dismissive hand. "Probably just another jogger. Sounds like you have an overactive imagination."

I shook my head. "I don't know. I'm thinking I should at least tell the police what I saw."

She straightened a row of handbags on the table. "That's what they get paid to do."

"I guess," I said. "I'm still worried about Max. He's not familiar with the area. I'm scared he won't be able to find his way back."

"I'm sure he'll be fine. Probably got turned around. He's probably sitting on your patio right now wondering where his breakfast is. Is he chipped?"

"Definitely." Mo and I had seen to that the minute we decided to keep him.

"Well, there you go. Quit your worrying."

"You're right. I'm just being a worrywart for nothing."

"How about a purse? I just got these in."

I glanced at the selection, my heart not really into shopping. "Maybe tomorrow."

"These are all the rage right now. They may not last until

tomorrow." She chuckled at her joke. So far, there were very few people browsing.

"I saw these yesterday and couldn't wait to get a closer look." Maybe a few minutes wouldn't hurt. I had texted Mo when I left Sarge's booth, but they weren't due back for another hour at least.

"Have at it." She gestured to the bags hanging at the back of the booth. "If you see anything you can't reach, let me know."

I nodded. "Thanks."

"You got a good spot in the temporary section. Not too far away from the pool, but not so close that you get the noise," she said.

"Temporary?" I inspected a bag I thought would make a splendid gift for Lizbeth's birthday, which we would celebrate next week when Mo and I returned home.

"Means you'll move on—like me. Unless you plan to stick around. If that's the case, Olive will move you to a different site." She waved her arm to the left. "That section of the park is for permanent residents. Permanents live here year-round." She then gestured to the right. "That other section over there is temporary campers. They rent a spot and stay for a week, a month, whatever. Then they move on."

"We're here until Friday. Guess we're temporaries." We'd stay temporaries if I had my way. I had no intention of living year-round away from my home and my friends. Traveling in an RV wasn't my idea anyway, but when my stepfather gifted it to us and Mo announced his retirement, I jumped on the idea—mainly to get Mo to retire. He'd been putting it off for ages.

"No matter to me. I treat all my customers the same. These are genuine leather. They normally sell for one hundred and twenty-five apiece. I can make you a deal if you buy two or more."

I held out two identical purses. "How much for both?"

She pulled a tiny calculator from her pocket. "Let me see. I can do seventy for both. I got a sweet deal from my distributor."

Lizbeth had taught me a thing or two about flea markets and garage sales. The first price was always negotiable, sometimes even the second. Even though I adored the cute purses, I didn't for a minute believe they sold for one hundred and twenty-five dollars each—even from a high-end boutique.

I pulled my credit card out of my pants pocket to show her I was serious. "How about forty for both?"

She scrunched her nose. "Hmm, I don't know. I'm already giving you an exceptional deal. They're designer, you know." She held out a bag. "Look at this leather."

I'd seen this same purse at one of the fancy department stores in the city. I'd never been willing to spend that kind of money on a purse before, but I always admired them.

"Let me think about it tonight." I slid the card back into my pocket and backed away from the booth.

"How about sixty?" she asked.

"Fifty," I countered.

"Fifty-five, and I'll throw in matching coin purses. Final offer."

I laughed. "Deal."

"Don't tell Sandi. She'll be over here trying to get a bargain."

After I went to the sheriff's department for fingerprinting, I headed back to the RV and arrived at the same time Mo showed up from his outing with Sandi's husband. Stan was a big, burly man with curly red hair. He had so many freckles he almost looked tan, but pale pink skin between his freckles screamed sunburn.

Mo made the introductions while he and Stan unloaded the car.

"We've got a cooler packed with fish. Hope you're ready for a tasty fish fry." Mo pecked me on the cheek. "Any sign of Max?"

"No. I handed out flyers at the flea market. There's a stack on the table for you."

"Let me get this stuff put away, then I'll take them around."

Stan set a cooler on the picnic table. "Hope you don't have plans tonight. We're fixing to have a fish fry."

He must have read the look of panic on my face. I hated cooking fish. In the enclosed space of a camper, I could imagine the odor lingering for days.

"Don't worry, we'll cook. At our place. I have a big kettle I put on the grill over a roaring fire. So the fish doesn't smell up the RV. Learned that lesson a long time ago." Stan laughed, and dimples as deep as craters appeared on his speckled cheeks. "The wife used to hate frying up a mess of fish. Now she loves it almost as much as I do, especially since I cook. All she has to do is whip up a few sides."

"Whatever, as long as I don't have to clean them," I said.

Mo put his arm around me and gave me a squeeze. "Nope. We cleaned, filleted, and packed them in ice down at the dock."

Bless his heart.

"Bet your new knife came in handy." I smiled a hopeful smile.

Mo's cheerful face, the face I loved to wake up next to every morning, turned sad, and my hopeful smile disappeared, along with my appetite.

"About the knife," Mo said.

"You lost it?" I asked, already knowing the answer.

"Misplaced. Don't worry. I'll find it."

Not likely. "How could you lose it?" Normally this would

not come as a surprise. Mo misplaced stuff all the time, but this situation was different. The freaking knife was a murder weapon, and my husband was the last one to have it.

"Calm down, hon. It's around here somewhere. I didn't realize it was missing until I was on the boat. Stan pulled out a similar one to cut some fishing line, and that's when I realized I didn't have it. I haven't checked the pants I wore yesterday."

"Stan has one like it?" I almost burst into song.

"Yeah, his has a heron on the handle," Mo said.

Just like that, my balloon of happiness burst. "Big deal."

"It'll turn up." Mo stopped. "Wait, I left it on the picnic table. It never made it to my pocket. I'll check the ground; I must have knocked it off."

Yeah, I thought. *The knife isn't the only thing that got knocked off.*

"Looks like it's time for me to leave. See you tonight." Stan jogged across the grass between our RVs, waving as he went.

"Yeah," I said, a little too snippy. "See you tonight."

"How was your day?" Mo changed the subject. He was good at redirecting my anger. Only, I wasn't angry. I was terrified. "I figured if Max hadn't turned up, it might be nice for you to meet Stan's wife since they're right next door. How was yoga? Did you and Cal work things out?" Mo sat at the picnic table.

"I met Stan's wife at yoga. She reminded me of Lizbeth." How was I going to tell Mo about the knife? We had planned this vacation as a relaxing time to celebrate his retirement. Instead, his knife was used to murder someone. The knife I bought him. I knew without a doubt he'd go all police chiefy on me. I could hear him now. *If you knock and don't get an answer, leave. Why did you go inside Cal's? Mind your own business, Mattie. Let the police figure this out.*

"Mo, there's something you need to know," I said.

"Yeah?"

"Cal's dead."

I'd wanted to tell him about his knife being the murder weapon while dancing around the part about me actually being at the murder scene when her body was discovered. At least that was the plan until I saw a police car coming down the street.

The car rolled to a stop at the curb. Deputy Beau unfolded himself from the cruiser and strolled toward us.

Mo's mouth still hung open. "What?" he finally asked. "What did you say?"

Deputy Beau walked up to Mo and extended a hand. "Mr. Modesky, I presume."

Mo reached for the deputy's hand and shook it. "Yes, I'm Mo Modesky. What can I do for you, Deputy?"

"Your wife has some explaining to do." Deputy Beau shook his finger in my face. "You left out a very important detail when we talked earlier."

Mo looked from me to the deputy and took a step forward. "What is this all about?"

"Keep your distance, sir." The deputy stood his ground.

Mo didn't retreat. Instead, he held up his hand. "Calm down, young man, and tell me what's going on."

The deputy pulled out a plastic bag with the knife I'd seen sticking out of Cal's neck. "I believe this belongs to you."

Mo leaned in to inspect the evidence. "Can't say one way or another, Deputy."

"Is this your knife?" the deputy repeated.

"Again, Deputy, I can't say it is or it isn't." Mo didn't give an inch.

The deputy shook the bag in front of me. "Is this the knife you purchased from Sterling Thorne at the flea market yesterday?"

"Who?" I asked.

"Sarge."

I shrugged.

The deputy pulled a knife from his pants pocket. It looked identical to the knife in the bag, except it had a sheriff's star carved into the handle. "I know where the knife came from. I talked to Sarge, who said he sold you the eagle knife yesterday, Mrs. Modesky. Is this the knife you bought from Sarge?"

"Look, I bought a knife from him yesterday. Now whether that's the one I bought, I couldn't tell you." Being a cop's wife had taught me a couple of things. The first was never to admit anything.

"Mrs. Modesky, I'm going to need you to come down to the station with me."

Mo's face turned scarlet. "Mattie, what is going on?"

Words wouldn't come. I gulped. "I . . . I . . ."

"Mrs. Modesky," the deputy said.

"Now, just a minute, young man. She's not going anywhere. If that is my knife, and I'm not saying it is, I was the last one to see it. You want someone to come with you, then I'll go down to the station with you until we get this straightened out. But you leave my wife out of this."

My heart sank.

"Be my guest," Deputy Beau said.

"Him? No." A feeling of panic shot through me. "He didn't do anything. I—"

"Mattie, shut up," Mo said.

I heard the fear in his voice. In over forty years, he'd never once told me to shut up, and he'd never used a tone that made my own fear ratchet so rapidly.

"But—"

"Mattie, *stop*."

"I'm waiting, Mr. Modesky," Deputy Beau said.

When Mo didn't respond, the deputy pulled out a pair of handcuffs and dangled them from his finger. "We can do this peacefully, or we can do it the hard way."

Mo looked at me. "Those will not be necessary. I'm a

retired law officer. I'll be happy to come down to the station. Mattie, call Jay Brent."

I watched as the deputy followed Mo to the car. My heart beat so rapidly, I thought I was having a heart attack. "Breathe slowly, Mattie," I told myself, trying my best to calm down. "Breathe. Take a deep breath and slowly let it out." Why did I buy that stupid knife? Why hadn't I told Mo the whole story? Why had Mo so selflessly gone with Deputy Beau? It should be me. Despite forcing myself not to hyperventilate, my mind raced through scenarios where Mo did not have an alibi. Or me. I didn't have one either. Other than Sarge seeing me for a short period of time, I'd not seen or talked to anyone until Mo came home. And who knew how long he'd been out searching for Max. We were doomed. My fingers fumbled over the screen while I tried to find Jay Brent's number. It took five tries before I finally tapped the right digits and the line for the best criminal attorney in the state began to ring.

CHAPTER SEVEN

I searched every inch of the RV for the stupid knife. Back home, I had a decorative dish on our dresser. At night Mo cleaned out his pants pockets and deposited everything in the dish. We'd had more than one quarrel about me washing his cell phone in the laundry when he hadn't emptied his pockets. Now it was routine. The RV had no dresser. Everything was built in. Since last night was our first night in the motor home, I didn't even know where or if Mo had emptied his pockets.

The outside search didn't go any better. I checked on and under the picnic table, the side table by our lawn chairs, the grill, and came up empty-handed.

I even called Lizbeth and relayed the whole incident to her. She suggested checking the chair cushions, which I had already done. And the fridge didn't have a top. At least not one where we could put anything.

When we disconnected, someone knocked on the door. It was well after five. I rushed to the door thinking it might be Mo, but he wouldn't have knocked. Unless he'd misplaced his key.

I pulled the curtain aside and saw Sandi standing on the concrete pad. When I opened the door, she rushed in.

"O-m-g, I heard about your husband." She pulled me into a hug. "I wanted to shut down the booth, but I just couldn't. The minute I closed, I hurried over. Are you okay? Is he okay?"

Tears built up behind my eyelids, but I willed them away. Now was not the time to be weak or show weakness. I didn't really know Sandi. Other than she seemed nice and reminded me of Lizbeth.

I pulled away. "What are you doing here? How did you know about Mo?"

"Stan called me when he saw Mo get in the back of the police car. He was standing at the sink and saw the whole thing through the window." Sandi led me to the sofa. "Sit down. Let me make you a cup of tea. Do you even drink tea?"

I nodded and motioned to the cabinet next to the refrigerator.

"When we found Cal, did you know that was Mo's knife?" She took two cups from the dish drainer and nuked water for the tea.

I hesitated. How did she know it was Mo's knife? Part of me wanted to spill out everything I knew, like I had done with Lizbeth, but I held back. "I don't know that it's his knife. How do you even know about it?"

"I was in my booth next to Sarge when Deputy Beau came calling. He told Sarge he recognized the knife because he bought one from Sarge a while back." Sandi set a cup on the table beside me and took an adjacent seat. "He pressed Sarge for details on who bought the knife, and Sarge gave him your name. Told him you had purchased it for your husband."

I rubbed my temples, trying to massage away a headache. "This whole thing is a mess. Mo would never hurt anyone. That is just not in his nature. And other than meeting Cal yesterday for a short time, we didn't know her." I dipped the tea bag a few times then pulled it out.

"Stan said he saw her over here yesterday after you checked in."

"Yeah, she stopped by with a store-bought pie claiming she'd made it especially for Mo." I cringed, remembering the encounter.

"Ah, the old pie ruse. She pulled that on Stan too."

"Mo is so naïve in the woman department." Mo and I had been together since high school—a long time. He had never dated anyone else, and neither had I. Even during college, we'd stayed connected through letters, phone calls, and visits to each other's campuses. "He suggested it might be nice for me to become friends with her. That maybe she was lonely, and some female companionship might put an end to her trying to seduce all the menfolk."

Sandi chuckled. "Did you? Befriend her?"

"Nope. Never saw her again until we found her." I knew how it would sound if I told Sandi I had gone to Cal's last night to tell her to stay away from Mo.

"Well, what are we going to do to help your husband?" Sandi leaned in, rubbing her hands together.

"What?" Why was she so willing to help? For all I knew, she could have killed Cal. That would get Cal off her back about the flea market. Or maybe Cal had come on to Sandi's husband one too many times. Or was she worried her own husband might be involved? Was this her way of trying to get information to make Mo look guilty and take the heat off her or Stan?

"We can't leave this up to Deputy Beau. No offense, he's a great guy and good at what he does, but that department is underfunded, understaffed, and overwhelmed. The drug problem in this county is eating away at all of their resources. I'm thinking the murder of an almost eighty-year-old woman who had a habit of going after married men will not be on their priority list. Next week, most of us will be gone—all except the permanent residents—then the suspect list shrinks. They will either pin this on your husband, or if that doesn't stick, it will go in a pile on a desk somewhere with all their other unsolved cases."

My mouth gaped open. "Do they have a lot of unsolved cases?"

"Oh, that was a figure of speech. I don't know if they do or not, but I know they run themselves ragged trying to keep up with the drug trafficking. It only makes sense that they'd shelve Cal's case if they don't solve it right away. Can't afford to waste their precious resources. They turn a blind eye to everything else that goes on in this RV park." Sandi covered her mouth. "Oops, shouldn't have said that."

"It's out there now. What do you mean by everything else that goes on?" I wasn't buying her willingness to help.

"The everyday drama. That kind of stuff. There have been some petty thefts. Nothing terrible. Nothing like murder." Sandi paused for a sip of tea.

"Stan and I have been coming here for years, so we know all the permanent residents. Well, I do. Stan fishes every day. He rarely makes friends with anyone. In fact, it surprised me he took up with your husband so quickly."

Why did he get so friendly with Mo? I went to the cabinet and found the batch of gooey butter cookies Lizbeth had made for me. "How about a cookie to go with that tea?" I asked. The kitchen in this thing was impressive for being an RV. I had just about everything I needed to cook while we were on the road. I hadn't skimped when it came to stocking the place. Cooking for Mo was one of my favorite pastimes, and he was a willing guinea pig for my culinary experiments.

"I never turn down a cookie." Sandi snatched one off of the plate even before I set it on the table. "These look amazing. Did you make them?"

"My friend Lizbeth. She's quite the baker." I returned to

my seat. "It doesn't surprise me about Mo and your husband at all. Mo is an outgoing person. He knows no strangers. People always feel comfortable around him. It's just his nature." I broke a cookie in half and popped it into my mouth.

"Stan is shy. Well, not really shy. He's an introvert. Once he gets to know you, you can't shut him up, but it's the getting-to-know part, because he rarely makes the first move." She stopped and laughed. "Don't tell Stan I told you this because it embarrasses him, but I asked him out first. He beat around the bush so long, I got tired of waiting. I finally walked right up to him and told him I wanted a date with him."

"How long have you two been together?" Sandi looked around my age, give or take a couple of years. But Stan was hard to tell.

"Had our thirtieth anniversary last month. But we've been together over forty years. Neither one of us was in a hurry to get married. One morning we decided, what the heck, neither one of us was going anywhere so why not get married. Drove ourselves to the courthouse and, *voilà*, the rest is history." Sandi waved her hands in a flourish, like a conductor conducting a symphony.

Our conversation came so easily, I almost forgot about Mo. I glanced at my watch.

"What are we going to do?" Sandi asked.

I narrowed my gaze. "What do you mean?"

"About your husband, of course. We can't just sit around waiting. We need to figure out who did this and why." Sandi's eyes lit up like a kid about to open the biggest present under the Christmas tree.

"Why do you want to help?"

The grin on Sandi's face disappeared. "I just thought I could help."

The thought of digging into this intrigued me, especially

since Mo had been hauled away for questioning. But Sandi's suggestion only increased my suspicion of her and Stan.

What would Lizbeth do? She'd tell me to keep an eye on Sandi. What better way than to go along with her plan.

"I don't even know where to begin." I thought for a minute. "We need to compile a suspect list." I pulled a sheet of paper off my grocery pad and grabbed a pen. "I'm afraid the only people I've even met are Olive, Ruby, Kat, Sarge, and you. Oh, and I've met Stan." Sandi knew all those people better than me, so her input would be valuable. If she really could be trusted. If not . . . well, I didn't plan to share anything important with her until I knew her motivation.

"You know your husband, and I know all the dirt around here. Between the two of us, we can figure this out," Sandi said.

I listed each person I had met since we'd been here. "Let's start with Olive. I know she seemed aggravated with Cal. I'm sure as the manager she gets complaints about her. But that's not enough to kill someone, is it?" I asked.

Sandi made a waffling gesture with her hand. "I know Olive has fielded a lot of complaints. She's a petty person, but Cal has ramped up her complaints about the flea market this year. She's taken it upon herself to be the flea market police. You heard her yesterday with me. No one has escaped her wrath."

"Olive manages the flea market too?" I couldn't imagine gentle Olive running this whole place single-handedly.

"Not just the manager, honey. She owns the whole deal. Her husband used to run the flea market, and Olive ran the park part, but he passed a couple of years ago. Olive is too tight to hire anyone to run the flea market. She does it all herself. This place used to be a showplace, but lately it's suffering from neglect. Cal's bickering with booth owners isn't helping. We used to have ten times as many booths as we do now. Same with the RV park. Stan used to make reservations months in advance. Now we can drive in with no notice and get a good spot."

"Olive stays on the list," I said.

"Agreed. With Cal gone, she gets rid of two headaches."

"What about Ruby?" I asked.

"You saw how she was this morning. Who knows what family secrets were between her and Cal? She needs to be on the list."

"What do you know about Kat?"

"She's a tough one. All work." Sandi frowned. "Other than coming for yoga, she's a loner. If Kat isn't in her booth, we rarely see her."

I tapped the paper. "Motive?"

"Kat and Cal had it out at the flea market. A pretty public blow-up," Sandi said.

"About her booth or something else?"

"Beats me. I didn't actually witness it, but Olive did."

"Kat stays on the list."

Sandi held up her cup. "How about more tea?"

While I refreshed our teas, Sandi's cell rang, and she answered it. I stayed by the sink with the pretense of giving her privacy. Though, privacy in an RV was not to be had. At least, I hadn't found a way short of locking myself in the bathroom and running water full blast into the sink.

Mo still had not returned, nor had I heard from him. The attorney had, had plenty of time to make it there. What was taking so long? If they arrested Mo, they had to let him call me.

Sandi disconnected from her call. "Sorry, that was Olive wanting to know details. She likes to keep her finger on what's going on."

"Why'd she call you?" Another reason to be suspicious. None of these people knew me and Mo. Yet, they all knew one another.

"There are no secrets here. Everyone knows everyone

else's business. One of the residents who was milling around must have seen us outside Cal's this morning and called Olive. All of these hens want to be the first to spread the bad news. Now where were we on the list?"

"We've got Olive, Ruby, and Kat. What about Sarge?" I purposely left her and Stan's names off my list, but I kept them in my mind. If it turned out Mo's knife was the murder weapon, it wasn't a random coincidence. Someone had found Mo's knife. Stan and Sandi were as good of suspects as anyone. One of them could have seen the knife lying on the picnic table and helped themselves. "Sarge seems nice."

He hadn't convinced me his knives were one of a kind. If there were others out there, I needed to find them. If I could find even one duplicate, it would prove they weren't unique.

"Here's the thing about Sarge. He takes Cal out once a week for dinner. The rumor mill around here thinks he's seeing someone else. And it's not Cal. But no one has ever seen him with anyone. He doesn't take part in poker night or any of the fishing events. The only time we see him is if he's out running or working in his booth. Otherwise, he's not around." Sandi took another cookie and broke it in half. She wagged a piece at me. "If I tell you something, you promise not to tell?"

"Ha! Who would I tell?"

"I think it's Ruby, but she denies it. I haven't asked Sarge." The cookie disappeared in her mouth. Crumbs had fallen onto her T-shirt. She brushed them onto the table, then scooted them into a pile. "That would make Cal good and mad."

"If that's true, that would put both of them right up at the top of the list, especially since Cal was so possessive of Sarge." I tapped the pen on the suspect list then drew a line between Ruby and Sarge. One more motive for Ruby. And Sarge too.

Sandi reached over and took my list. "That pretty much

wraps it up. No one else in the park had as much to gain with Cal gone. I mean, she was a nuisance, but not enough to kill her."

"Do any of them run besides Sarge?" That individual may or may not have killed Cal, but they were the last to see Max. I needed to find out who it was. For Max and for Mo.

I'd been so caught up after Mo left with the deputy that I hadn't thought about Max. Fear for him rose again in my gut, and suddenly I wished I was out looking for him, not inside looking at a list of suspects.

"Run? Like jogging?" Sandi hooted with laughter. "Not hardly. What's that got to do with anything?"

"My dog didn't just run away." I reminded her about seeing Sarge when I was walking Max and later how we'd seen someone outside of Cal's. "Sarge had already gone home or at least said he did. But Max took off after whoever it was, and I haven't seen him since." Tears threatened to come, and I bit my lip trying to keep from crying.

"Oh, Mattie." Sandi reached across the table and patted my hand. "He'll come home. With all the flyers you're putting up, someone will recognize him."

I sniffed and swiped at my eyes. "Sorry, I hate getting all emotional."

"Don't worry about it."

"How's Scooter settling in?"

Sandi rolled her eyes. "He whined most of the night. This morning I found him curled up next to Stan. Hopefully, we'll figure out what to do with him before Stan gets attached. Or me. I'll be the one who gets attached. That dog is so darn cute."

"Oh, hey, did you go by for your fingerprints?" I asked.

Sandi smacked her forehead. "Crap! I totally forgot. I'll go tomorrow or else Deputy Beau will come and haul me off."

Outside, a car door slammed. I hoped against hope it was Mo.

A few seconds later the door opened, and he walked in. His shoulders sagged like he carried an enormous weight. He hadn't shaved this morning, and his whiskers were already well past a five o'clock shadow.

"Hey, hon." He bent and kissed me on the cheek. "Who's your friend?"

Sandi's face lit up in a smile. "I'm Stan's wife, Sandi." She hooked her thumb at the RV parked next to us. "Your neighbor."

"Ah, sorry about screwing up the fish fry," Mo said. "Maybe we can do it tomorrow."

Sandi nodded. "No worries. We'll figure it out. I better go. Stan will worry if I'm not home."

"I'm going to hop in the shower and freshen up." Mo disappeared into the bedroom.

I walked Sandi to the door.

"We don't have yoga in the morning since it's Sunday, but if you want to go for a walk, I'm game. I have to go early since the flea market opens at eight," she said. "We can talk more about our suspects." She laughed and let herself out.

"Don't forget those fingerprints," I called to her retreating back.

CHAPTER EIGHT

"Are you ready to talk about what happened today?" Mo and I sat outside after we'd finished a quick dinner of leftover bratwurst. The men had rescheduled the fish fry for tomorrow.

"Nothing to talk about." Mo took a swig of his beer. "I sat around twiddling my thumbs until Jay arrived. Once he got there, they questioned me. Then I sat around some more. Finally, they told me to go home. Jay dropped me off here and headed home."

"That's it?"

"Yup." Mo tilted his bottle and drained it. "You want another?"

"Heavens, no. I'll be up all night as it is." Beer was not my beverage of choice. I wasn't an anything drinker really, but Mo loved a beer to cap off the day, so I figured I would indulge. One was my limit.

"What did you do all day?" Mo returned with another beer and twisted off the cap. He handed me a bag of chips.

Normally that question would irk me. Mo used to ask me that all the time when he worked, like he couldn't see I'd cleaned the house or made an amazing dinner or washed all the dirty laundry. Tonight, it made me sad. We should be spending our time together. Instead, he'd been sitting in an interview room at the sheriff's department while I fretted.

"Took flyers around to the flea market," I said. "Since you were gone most of the day, I took them around to all the campsites. Did you talk to your friend at the sheriff's department while you were there?"

"Yeah, they'll keep an eye out for Max. Looks like you and Stan's wife were getting along pretty good. Does that mean we're going to finish out the week?"

I glanced at my fitness tracker. Four thirty had come and gone. "How can you even ask that with Max missing? I'm not leaving until we have him back. Besides, we're kind of stuck here now, aren't we?"

"No, the deputy knows how to contact me. We do need to find Max. I would really like to go out on the boat again tomorrow with Stan."

My hopes soared. "Does that mean they cleared you?"

"No, still a suspect. Let's play cards." He said it so matter-of-factly.

"Play cards? How can you play cards when you're still a suspect? Did you tell them you're a retired police chief?"

"Of course. In fact, I know the sheriff. That's who I had the beer with. We went to the police academy together, and we used to see one another at leadership training sessions at the state patrol office. But this is a murder investigation. Until I'm off the hook, so to speak, I'm still a suspect."

"Why am I not a suspect? I bought the knife, and I'm the one who found Cal. Well, me and Sandi. This is beyond ridiculous."

"Mattie, don't say that. Don't even think about it. You hear me?" Mo's eyebrows drew together. "You didn't discuss this with her, did you?"

"Are you kidding me? Why would you think I would discuss it with Sandi?" I could not hide the indignation I felt.

Mo didn't even crack a grin. "I know you, that's why. Now did you?"

I didn't say anything.

"I knew it. Well, don't say anything else. This is between us. You and me. I better run that flyer over to the sheriff's department. I'll take another drive around the park while I'm out." Mo stood and dropped his bottle into the trash can.

"I'm going to see if I can catch Olive and ask her to print more flyers," I said. "I wish I'd never bought that stupid knife."

"And I wish I'd put it away or put it in my pocket. Or even remember what I did with it." Mo laughed. "But we can't dwell on that. Chin up, hon. We both know I'm innocent. Let's concentrate on finding Max while the sheriff's department figures this all out."

"I know." I forced a smile.

"Any news on your dog?" Olive asked when I walked in the door. "I saw your flyers at the flea market."

"Not a word. Would you mind if I made some more? I'll be glad to reimburse you."

Olive waved a hand in the air. "Don't worry about it. You make all you need. Come around this side of the counter and help yourself."

I settled in front of the copy machine and went to work. "Thanks."

"Did you find any bargains while you were there?"

I looked up. "A couple of purses, but my heart wasn't really into shopping."

"Did you check out the nut booth? They give out samples and have the best pecans."

"Nope." The paper jammed, and I pulled out the tray to straighten the paper.

Olive continued to flit around, making small talk. I felt confident Sandi had told her about Mo being at the sheriff's department. I wondered if her easy conversation wasn't a way to warm up to asking me about it. "Mo didn't do it," I finally said in my best deadpan voice.

Olive's hand flew to her mouth. "I never for an instant thought he did."

"Good, because he didn't." A streak of stubbornness that I could not explain overtook me. "Apparently it's not as safe here as everyone would like to think."

"I can assure you nothing like that has ever happened at Oldies but Goodies. Nothing. Everyone here is beyond reproach." Olive's voice quivered as she talked. "I do not tolerate tomfoolery of any nature."

"Tell that to the person I saw sneaking around Cal's place last night while I was walking Max." I pulled the warm flyers from the copier tray and retrieved my original. "They might not have been up to tomfoolery, but they were up to something."

"Deputy Beau never said a word about someone sneaking around. If he had any suspicion we were still in danger, he would have warned me." Olive opened the gate in the counter and let me through.

"I failed to mention it to Deputy Beau, but I think I should. It could help."

"Probably should, if you think it will help find out who—" Olive shook her head. "I can't even stand to say it out loud."

"Thanks for letting me make these." I noticed she hadn't hung a flyer in the office. "Do you mind if I put one on the door?"

"Go ahead. I can't believe I didn't think to do that." She tore off a piece of tape and handed it to me. "One more thing."

"Yes." I stuck the flyer to the glass door and turned.

"Can you not be spreading rumors about seeing someone

messing around? I don't need the residents getting in an uproar."

I gave a noncommittal shrug, pushed through the door, and headed off to distribute more flyers. When I had gone door to door the first time, six of the RVs' occupants were out and about, so I'd not been able to talk to them. I made a second trip to follow up on the flyer and ask them in person if they'd seen Max. After all negative responses, my mood sank, and I returned to our RV. Max was still not there. Neither was Mo. But a note sticking in the door caught my attention, raising my hopes that someone had information on Max.

They did.

Sort of.

I HAVE YOUR DOG. HE'S FINE AND HIDDEN IN A SAFE SPOT. KEEP YOUR MOUTH SHUT. I'LL SEND INSTRUCTIONS ON WHERE TO FIND HIM. IF YOU GO TO THE COPS, HE'S MINE.

Cut out letters from a magazine were glued to a sheet of paper. The paper had a black-and-white photo of Max. He was lying with his face on his paws, looking like he'd lost his best friend.

CHAPTER NINE

Sandi was standing on the sidewalk doing stretches when I walked outside the next morning. "Do you need to stretch or are you okay?"

"I'm as limber as I'm going to get." I had the folded ransom note in my pocket. The note confirmed that Cal's killer had Max. I had almost told Mo when he came home last night, but he'd doubled down on telling me to mind my business about Cal's death and let the authorities work it out. He had shown no interest in getting involved. Since he was still a suspect with no alibi, I felt more determined than ever to clear his name and find Max in the process.

Showing him the note would only make him feel more strongly about it, and then I'd never find my dog.

Walking with Sandi allowed me to get to know her better and decide if she was a suspect or a friend. Until then I'd keep the ransom note to myself. Also, if someone in the park had Max, they'd eventually have to bring him outside to potty. I could keep my eyes open for him or listen for his barks as we walked. After Mo had gone to bed, I'd gone over the image in the note with Mo's magnifying glass to see if I could see anything that would help determine where he was being held. The blurry background told me nothing.

We walked at a brisk pace for the first twenty minutes. Sandi was a dynamo, and I had a hard time keeping up. "Jeez, you didn't tell . . . me you were . . . a power walker." My breath hitched as I tried to get the words out.

"Sorry, we can slow down." Sandi eased her pace.

"Thanks. I'm used to walking every morning with Lizbeth, but nothing like this. You walk a lot faster than I'm used to." I stopped to let my breathing catch up.

We had walked every street in the temporary section and were just starting in the permanent section.

"Hey, is that Olive?" I asked.

"Where?" Sandi looked around, trying to catch a glimpse of the park manager.

"Right there." I pointed to an adorable yellow park model with latticework around the base and a huge porch on the front with an attached carport.

The woman in question had left via the side door that exited onto the carport and was making her way along a line of bushes at the back of the unit.

"Oh, my Lordy. That's Sarge's place, and that *is* Olive." Sandi cut through the next lot, and I followed.

"I thought so," I said, trying to catch up.

"Not so loud." Sandi crept through a break in the hedge and squatted. She grabbed my hand and pulled me down.

"What's going on? Why all the cloak and dagger?" I asked.

"Because it's Olive," Sandi said. "And that is where Sarge lives."

"So?" I stared at Olive's retreating figure, not making the connection.

"Do I have to draw you a picture? Because it would be X-rated, if I did." Sandi chuckled.

"She's the manager. She probably went to see him about business," I said.

Sandi scoffed. "Like monkey business. It's Sunday. The office doesn't even open until ten. And she doesn't live here. She lives in town. There's only one reason Olive would be at Sarge's place."

I finally got the full impact of what Sandi meant. "Oh, you mean . . . What's wrong with that? Who cares?"

Sandi put her finger to her lips. "Shh! Come on." She stayed in a crouched position and duckwalked along the hedge.

"Are you serious?" I stood up. "My knees will kill me if I do that."

"Get down. And follow me."

I kneeled instead of the crouched position and followed along. My knees would still kill me, but if I crouched and duckwalked, I'd likely need a crane to get up or a knee replacement. While I had ample padding everywhere else, my knees did not. I quickly caught up to Sandi.

"Where are we going?" I asked.

"To see where she's going." Sandi pointed to Olive, who meandered along the other side of the hedge like she was out for a morning stroll.

What was I thinking? She probably stopped by Sarge's to bring him a coffee cake. Or stopped by for a morning quickie. Good for her.

"What makes you so sure she's up to something?" I asked.

Olive stopped at the chain-link fence that separated the RV park from the main road. She pulled open a section of the fence and slipped through.

"That! That is why I think she's up to something." Sandi stood up and race-walked to the fence. "That and the rumor going around that Sarge has a secret girlfriend. Keep up."

I pulled myself to my feet. Not a simple task. It felt like doing a deep knee bend in reverse. I was severely allergic to anything requiring me to get on my knees. The result usually brought on a severe sweat followed by the need for an ice pack, a couple of pain relievers, and a glass of wine—not necessarily in that order.

When I caught up, Sandi pulled the fence aside, and we went through.

"Where is she?" I asked.

Sandi pointed to the twenty-four-hour discount store across the street. Olive opened the door of a cranberry-colored SUV and got in.

"Now tell me she wasn't up to something." Sandi's smirk said she had caught Olive in a nasty transgression.

"You think she went to all the trouble of parking over there to keep from being caught?"

"The way rumors abound in this place, I'd say Miss Olive and Sarge are doing the horizontal tango, and she knows this place well enough to know she can't leave her car parked at the office overnight. Get down." Sandi grabbed my hand and pulled me down behind a cedar tree.

I lost my balance and went down hard on my tailbone. "Give me a little warning, will you? If I break a hip, it's on you." I sat in the grass, worrying about ticks and chiggers, but wanting to put on a brave front. Like Lizbeth, Sandi acted fearless. My middle name was Chicken, unless you messed with my family. That turned me into a grizzly bear.

We both watched as Olive drove off the lot and headed to town.

"You're going to have to get a lot tougher if you're going to hang with me." Sandi stood up, grabbed my hand, and pulled me to my feet.

"Tell me something I don't know." I brushed the grass off my yoga pants and checked my legs for ticks. I'd only had one of the creepy things in my entire life, and that was enough. Next time Sandi suggested a walk, I would spray down with insect repellant.

She pulled the fence aside.

"Don't let that snag my top. It's new." I bent over to squeeze through.

When we were on the other side, we retraced our steps. This time without the crouching and crawling. My knees and back appreciated the relief.

"Why does anyone care what Olive does or who she does it with?" I asked.

"Olive is Miss Prim and Proper. You saw how Cal acted around your husband. Cal and Ruby have quite the reputation and have never tried to hide it. Besides, neither one of them is from around here. Olive lives here. She grew up here. Her late husband was the mayor. From what I understand, she's a retired teacher and protective of her reputation. Plus, she's a widow. She would die at any hint of scandal."

"Whoa, for being a temporary resident, you're sure up on the local gossip." This place sounded like my hometown of Pine Grove. I was beginning to think all small towns were the same—rumor central.

"What can I say? Running a flea market booth is akin to being a bartender or a hairdresser. Only the customers aren't talking to me. It's like I'm invisible. People browse and talk. I listen. Sometimes I hear good stuff. Sometimes I hear about Aunt Gertie's gout. It's a trade-off."

When we got to the main road, we turned toward our street. Vendors were already arriving to open their booths for the day.

Sandi glanced at her fitness tracker. "Good grief. I gotta run. I need to take a shower and change. Let's do the fish fry tonight. You okay with that?"

Before I could answer, she sprinted off, leaving me standing with my mouth hanging open.

CHAPTER TEN

I reluctantly returned home, made myself a cup of tea, and went out on the patio to strategize my next move. A light breeze blew through the trees, bringing the promise of rain. I loved thunderstorms. But I worried about Max. He was fine at home, but being in a strange place without Mo and me would make him anxious. Not to mention being held captive by a stranger. I also worried about Mo being out on the water. Surely, the guys would have enough sense to come in at the first hint of rain.

Sandi walked by on the way to her booth and waved. Once she was out of sight, I ran inside, washed my cup, and put it in the drainer to dry.

Sitting and thinking about Max and Mo, I had worked myself into a lather of tension. I grabbed Max's extra leash. My helplessness in the situation could be resolved by doing something. Mo knew the dangers of being on the lake during a storm, so he could take care of himself, but Max was another story. Unless I chose to share the ransom note with Mo, and I had no intention of doing that, it was up to me to find Max. Sitting around on my duff worrying didn't do anyone any good.

I walked down to the flea market and back, then continued past our street, calling his name. Olive was pulling her car into the manager's space in front of the office. I wanted an opportunity to talk to her without Sandi around. I liked Sandi, but she and Stan were suspects until I found a reason for them not to be. For all I knew, she thought the same things about me and Mo. But, whatever. She didn't need to know everything I found out.

"Hi, Mattie." Olive shut the car door and adjusted her purse on her shoulder. "Any word on your dog?" She had changed from the outfit she'd had on when Sandi and I saw her leaving Sarge's place.

"Not yet. But I'm still asking around."

"Stick with it." She glanced at the sky. "Hopefully, he'll turn up before it storms."

"Do you think so?"

"You can hope, right? What's going to happen to Cal's little dog, Scooter?"

"Sandi took him home for the time being," I said. "Guess she'll figure that all out."

"Yeah, I can't see Ruby taking him. Besides, she has like a dozen cats. Definitely not a dog person."

If Ruby had Max, he'd be going nuts in a house full of cats. "What about you? Are you a dog person?"

"I love dogs. Wish I could have one," she said in a wistful tone.

Enough to steal one? "Why don't you?"

"My grandson is highly allergic. If he gets within breathing distance of a dog, his eyes water, the sneezing starts, and he's miserable."

No matter. Ruby and Olive both had motive, and I wasn't ready to rule either one of them out.

"Too bad. Max has been such a joy for Mo and me. I miss him terribly," I said.

Several cars passed, heading to the flea market, and most

of them honked or waved. Some yelled greetings as they passed.

"Morning, Olive."

"Hey, Olive. Hope we find some bargains today."

Olive waved back to each car. "Looks to be a busy day at the flea market."

"You seem to know everyone," I said.

"I've been doing this a lot of years. Didn't use to know so much about the flea market side of the biz. My husband always did that." Her eyes teared up. "But since he passed, I'm doing the best I can."

"Oh, I'm so sorry."

"I sure miss his handyman ways. I'm not nearly as good at keeping this place up as he was." Her voice tightened, and she cleared her throat before continuing, "Place is falling down around me. Some residents help now and then, but I don't feel right taking their charity, and I can't afford to pay them or discount their rent. So, I fix what I can when I can."

"I'm sure it can be overwhelming. There's a lot to take care of and so many personalities to deal with. That seems like a lot for anyone," I said.

"You can say that again. We have a lot of change with new people like you and your husband who come and go. It's refreshing meeting new people, making new friends. The permanent side is another matter. Good, bad, or indifferent, they are here to stay. Most everyone gets along. We get one or two who don't fit in with the crowd, and that causes trouble." She looked down at her feet.

"You mean Cal and Ruby?" I asked.

"Ruby, I can deal with by ignoring her. She's never been as overt as Cal. Cal, though. You cannot imagine the complaints I've gotten over the years." Olive patted the side of her face. "Whew! I hate to speak ill of her, but what can I do? It's not like flirting is against the law. At least she won't be harassing my folks at the flea market. Maybe some of my former booth owners will come back." She cupped her mouth. "Oh my, I didn't mean that to be as ugly as it sounded."

"Is there anything we can do for her sister?" I hadn't gotten off on a good foot with Ruby, but now was not a time to hold grudges. "Back home, when a loved one passed, the church ladies would make covered dishes for the family. Is there anyone here who organizes that sort of thing?"

Olive shrugged. "I'm not sure you'll rouse up much sympathy. In fact, it wouldn't surprise me if there weren't some happy campers—literally. Cal made no friends, and Ruby's personality is so toxic, most people steer clear of her."

My jaw dropped at her pronouncement. "That sounds so heartless. It makes me sad. What about the women who come to yoga?"

"The only reason Cal and Ruby run the yoga class is because no one else wants to get up in front of the group. They only learned about yoga from videos, but they know more than the rest of us." She patted her middle. "Besides, I've got more than enough to go around, and I sure don't want to display it in front of the class."

I honed in for her reaction to my next question. "What about Sarge?"

Her eyebrows pinched together. "What about him?"

"I'd heard he and Cal were an item."

Her eyes hardened. "No, I told you Cal was obsessed with Sarge. I can assure you he did not return the obsession."

"Oh, I thought—"

"You thought wrong." Olive turned and pulled a handful of envelopes out of the mailbox next to the entrance. "Don't believe everything Sandi tells you. She likes to stir stuff up, and that's a dangerous business to be in."

Her remark caught my attention. "Why?"

She thumbed through her mail. "What? I'm sorry. This pile of bills distracted me."

"You mentioned Sandi liked to stir stuff up, and it was a dangerous business to be in."

Olive chuckled. "When you get a bunch of old women together, it doesn't pay to be the one stirring the pot. Yikes! Did you think I meant something bad?"

Three more cars drove past, honking and waving. Olive waved back.

"No, I wasn't sure how to take it."

"Looks like the money will roll in at the flea market today. Hope I can eventually fill some of those empty booths," Olive said, changing the subject. She pulled a key from her pocket and stuck it into the lock. "I better get to work. Half a dozen people are checking out today. You let me know if you and your husband need anything."

"Will do."

"Pay no attention to my rambling," Olive said over her shoulder. "Everything going on around here addles my brain."

Before the door closed, I took a chance. "Olive?"

She turned around and grabbed the door before it slammed. "Yes?"

"We're having a fish fry at Stan and Sandi's tonight. Would you be interested? The guys are frying the fish they've caught, and the ladies are putting together some sides."

"That's nice of you to offer, but I think I'll pass," Olive said.

"Can I ask a question?"

"Sure."

"Did you ever consider getting remarried?" Now it was my turn to be embarrassed. "Wow, that came off sounding nosy. I didn't mean it to. I just meant . . . well, I can't imagine being without Mo, but I also think I would be terribly lonesome."

"The thought never crossed my mind, dear. I like my life

just the way it is. Men only complicate matters. Like toilet seats and dirty laundry and dinner decisions."

I could commiserate, but I'd put up with all those things. Though, not having to worry about a toilet seat left up in the middle of the night might be a consideration. I shook off the thought. "I better get going. I'm going to ask around and see if anyone has seen Max."

"Have you checked the trail?"

"What trail?" How had I missed that? I'd walked over this RV park numerous times.

Olive pointed to a wooded area that rimmed one side of the park. "Behind the pool. There's a small sign with an arrow marking the beginning of the trail. It used to be in a lot better shape, but the walkers and golf carts keep it passable. There's a rickety old barn off the path. The county has been trying to get the owner to tear it down for years. Your dog may have gone inside and can't get out."

Now she tells me. "Is it private property?"

She shrugged and cocked her head. "The trail and surrounding woods are part of the state forest system. The barn sits on private property, but no one pays attention. Kids used to party out there, but not so much anymore. It's not accessible from the main highway since the owner gated the entrance."

That trail consisted of two ruts barely distinguishable due to an overgrowth of weeds. To be fair the ruts showed signs of recent use as the weedy middle was matted down. Streaks of sunlight slanted across the forest floor. I knew it was a long shot, but the ransom note had said Max was hidden in a safe spot. I'd walked the entire RV park and not heard one peep from him. If the dognapper had hidden him, what better place than an abandoned barn. It didn't hurt to at least take a look. I shivered. Not sure if it was from the drop in temperature once I'd entered the shady copse of trees or because unkempt nature gave me the creeps. This place reminded me of all the horror movies I'd seen. The movies where the girl entered the woods the whole time the audience silently screamed for her not to go in.

I swallowed my nerves and continued walking, vaguely aware of the critters I might encounter. High on my list of undesirables were snakes, ticks, and chiggers, until I walked into a spider web stretched between two trees. I screamed like a little girl while batting the sticky web away from my face and praying the resident spider was not in residence at the time of my capture.

I was so focused on searching my anatomy for the spider that I almost missed the overgrown footpath, which led to a broken-down barbed wire fence. A battered DO NOT TRESPASS sign lay on the ground with a bevy of footprints crisscrossing it.

The courage that I'd summoned waned, but I stepped across the wire and headed down the path, determined to find my dog. If finding him meant I had to endure spider webs and trespassing, so be it. Up ahead I saw the old barn Olive told me about. *Rickety* was an understatement. One entire side had collapsed in on itself. The other looked like a strong wind would send it to the ground. On the peak of the remaining roof sat four turkey vultures, or buzzards, as Mo always called them. I picked up my pace, dodging the weeds, rusty farm implements, and uneven terrain. If I didn't sprain an ankle or worse, it would be a miracle. I envisioned breaking my leg and being unable to get help, then the vultures would pick my bones clean. My fingers found the phone in my pocket and gripped it. If I went down, at least I could call for help.

"Max! Here, boy. Max!" I shouted as I approached the ramshackle barn. "Max!"

I gritted my teeth and stuck my head inside the doorway. Because so much of the barn wood was missing or destroyed, light filtered in, making it easy to see. "Max!" A skittering noise inside caused goose bumps to rise on my arms. "Dog, if you're in here, you better come on out."

I stepped up and over the rotten timber, which served as a threshold. Once inside, I inspected my surroundings, peering overhead to make sure nothing above would come crashing down and make me dinner for the vultures. The entire back end of the barn lay in a heap of collapsed wood and beams. To my left, an abandoned hay wagon still contained the remnants of its final load. To my right, a series of stalls in various stages of disrepair brought back memories and smells of mucking stalls in my grandfather's barn back home—a job I despised and felt was beneath me as a teenager with more exciting activities on my mind.

"Max." I crept closer to the stalls, raising my voice and shuffling my feet to make noise. "Max."

A mouse skittered across the top of a stall door. If that was the worst thing I encountered, I'd count myself lucky. In the first stall, I tripped and fell face down into a pile of musty smelling straw. I rolled over and sat up, spitting bits of straw from my mouth. Out of the corner of my eye, I saw a plastic cottage cheese container. No, there were two containers. One was tipped on its side and the other upside down. That didn't make any sense. I kicked them and a few stray bits of something that looked like dog food rolled out. I crawled over for a closer inspection. It was kibble. Someone had fed an animal here.

"Max!" Feeling a morsel of hope, I checked the other stalls, looking for anything that would lead me to my dog. There were no signs of him.

"Max!" I searched the entire barn—the parts I could access —and finally left dejected. The thought of Max being here alone, scared, and abandoned broke my heart. Had Cal's killer hid Max here, then moved him. My hopes of finding him continued to diminish. If I couldn't locate him by Friday, I'd have to tell Mo about the ransom note, because there was no way I was leaving Oldies but Goodies until I found my dog.

CHAPTER ELEVEN

Mo had not returned by the time I dragged myself up the steps of the RV, panting like I'd run the last mile, which I had not. The sun had decided to grace me with its presence, so I changed into my swimming suit, donned a coverup, and grabbed my e-reader. On the way to the pool, I thought about Olive. She'd made it clear she wasn't a fan of Cal's. This morning proved a connection between Olive and Sarge, with Cal definitely in the middle. Perhaps a love triangle, which Olive did not admit. Instead of going to the pool just yet, I detoured by the flea market.

"Hey lady," Sandi called when she saw me approaching her booth. "You look like you're ready to relax."

"I am. Got a new book queued up and a bag full of good-ies. I left Mo a note. I'm hoping he'll join me at the pool when they get back."

Sandi checked her watch. "It's pretty late for them. I bet Stan talked him into going for breakfast. There's a little café Stan loves. Probably wanted to introduce Mo to the best biscuits and gravy this side of the Mississippi."

I groaned. "Seriously? That's the last thing Mo needs to get hooked on. He'll want to go there every morning. That man has not met a plate of biscuits and gravy he doesn't fall in love with."

"Don't complain. You won't have to cook breakfast every morning. Gives you more time for reading and swimming."

"Instead, I'll be letting out pants and replacing buttons when they pop off his shirt." I spotted a gorgeous bracelet on a display. "Did you make this? It's so colorful."

"I made everything here. That's what I do with my spare time while Stan is out fishing and stuffing his face at the café." Sandi pulled the bracelet down and handed it to me.

I placed it across my wrist and fastened the clasp.

"Hold it up to the sun and watch how it sparkles," she said.

"Nice. Now I have to have it. Maybe I'll save it to give to Lizbeth for Christmas."

"Your friend is one lucky duck. Makes me jealous. I've never had a bestie. Stan was military, and we moved all over. When he retired, we started RVing. Never put down roots in one place long enough."

I reached across the table and touched her arm. "We'll be RV besties."

Sandi laughed. "Yeah, until the end of the week."

"Where are you headed next?" I asked.

"We've got three weeks in Minnesota on the North Shore. It's gorgeous this time of year."

"We're going back home for a week. I think Mo said we're going to Wisconsin." I handed the bracelet back. "Sold. I'll take it."

She removed the price tag and wrapped the bracelet in a square of tissue paper. "We have a whole itinerary we stick to every year. This is kind of our home base. Our daughter and her family live close by. When they get free time, she brings my grands down for a swim."

"Do you actually have a home?"

"Yeah, that big hunk of metal parked next to yours. With

Stan being in the military, we never owned a home, just rented wherever we were. When he retired, we didn't want to tie ourselves to one place."

That thought made my stomach roil. Mo had talked about selling our house if we found out we enjoyed living in a motor home. "Wow, I can't even imagine not having my home to go back to."

"I never got used to one, so I didn't have to adapt. It's kind of freeing to know everything you own is always with you."

"Whatever you say." I tucked the bracelet into my pool bag. "I'm off to get some rays. Mo says we're on for the fish fry tonight. I thought I'd make a watermelon salad with feta and poppyseed dressing."

Three women walked up and started asking Sandi questions about the jewelry. I waved to her and told her I'd see her tonight.

When I passed Sarge's booth, he called to me. "Miss Mattie, you got a minute?"

At this rate, it would be noon and hot by the time I made it to the pool.

"Sure," I said.

Sarge walked around to the front of the booth. "Hey, I'm sorry again about the knife. I hope you understand I was in a bit of a pickle with the deputy."

I was still kicking myself for buying the stupid knife, but it wasn't his fault. Unless there was more than one. I crossed my fingers. "Sarge, are you sure that in all the time you've sold those knives there was only one eagle? Maybe one slipped through the cracks."

"I'd love to tell you there were more out there, but I can't. Even if my memory wasn't so hot, and it is, the maker numbers each knife." He went into the booth and brought out a book. "I keep track of each one I sell. The one I sold you had the mark 'eg1.' Now I didn't see the knife they pulled out of Cal, but I'm betting it had the same mark on it."

"And I'm guessing you gave the police that mark?" I'd felt good about rounding up so many suspects, but with everything pointing to Mo, my mood took a tumble.

He nodded. "Yes, ma'am. I'm a firm believer of doing the right thing, even if sometimes it has the wrong consequences."

I hung my head.

"Don't be so glum. I'm sure there's a good explanation, and the truth will prevail."

"We can hope. Any chance you've seen my dog?"

He shook his head. "Sorry, but I've been keeping my eyes open."

I gave a half-hearted wave and continued on my way when a thought occurred to me. I trotted back before a customer could interrupt. "Mo and I are going to a fish fry with Sandi and her husband tonight. Any chance you and Mrs. Sarge would care to join us?"

"That's kind of you, but I'll take a pass," Sarge said.

"Oh, don't be like that." I jostled his arm. "Ask your wife and see. I'm sure she'd be grateful not to have to cook tonight. She doesn't even have to bring a dish. We've got everything covered."

Sarge's cheeks pinked. "I'm not married."

I took a deep breath and let it out. "No worries. If you're seeing someone, bring her. The more the merrier."

"Nope, it's just me." Sarge walked back into his booth and began fiddling with the merchandise.

"A handsome man like you?" I pushed. "Surely you have a special lady in your life."

"No, ma'am." He winked. "Now if you were available, Miss Mattie, I might just have to change my bachelorhood ways."

O-m-g! Is he flirting? I laughed. "I'm a one-man woman, Sarge. Mo and I have been together over forty years."

"If you ever consider a little hanky-panky on the side, call me." Sarge winked again.

Oh, my Lord, I couldn't tell if he was joking or serious. He'd been so polite the last time I'd talked to him. Or was it me? Did he think I was flirting? I was trying to be nice. It was a good thing he declined my invitation. Mo had never had to defend my honor, but I didn't want to see what would happen if he did. Mo was as even-tempered as they came, but he also didn't pander to philanderers.

CHAPTER TWELVE

I walked all the way to the pool, convincing myself Sarge hadn't flirted. Who gets hit on when they're sixty-four for goodness' sake? I was a grandmother. Lord, I hadn't flirted with another man—ever. Mo was my first love and my last. I hadn't looked at another man since seventh grade. I mean, Mo still made me feel all giggly and girly when I wasn't mad at him for something, but a man who wasn't Mo—holy moly. Part of me felt a tad excited. Not excited because I was looking. I was not someone like Ruby or Cal. But excited like when I bought a bottle of wine for my card club and the clerk asked to see my identification. I had felt giddy. Then the smart aleck had to spoil it by telling me he had to card everyone because he had to enter the birth date for the cash register to ring up. *Stupid little squirt!* At least he could have let me revel in it for a minute before crushing my spirit.

I spread my towel on a lounge chair and settled in with my e-book. A few chapters in, Mo arrived decked out in swim trunks carrying a towel and a cooler.

"Hey, pretty lady, you got an extra chair for me?" He swooped down and kissed me on the forehead.

"I don't think so. My husband might get jealous," I teased back. "He's got a temper."

A couple sitting on the edge of the pool turned and stared at us.

"Don't even joke about that," Mo said. "At least not here."

I waved at the couple. "Nothing to see here."

Mo grabbed my hand. "You are bad, woman. How about I rub some of that suntan lotion on you?"

His forehead, nose, and the tips of his ears were bright red.

"You're the one who needs sunscreen," I said.

"That stuff's for sissies. Besides, I need to get my tan on." He wiggled his pale legs in the air.

I slapped a leg. "Put that down. The paleness is blinding me."

"Have you seen that deputy sniffing around?" Mo asked.

"I haven't been paying attention. Why?" I asked.

"Stan said the guy was looking for Sandi." Mo reached into the cooler and pulled out two cold soft drinks. "He was waiting at Stan's when we got back. You want one?"

I nodded. "My guess is he wanted to check when she was going to come in to have her fingerprints taken." Before Mo could ask, I lifted my fingers in the air. "Already done. In other news, Sandi and I went for a walk this morning and saw something strange."

Mo unscrewed the caps and handed a bottle to me. "What?"

I hesitated.

"Go on, snoopy. I know you won't let this go." Mo tilted the bottle up and took a long swig.

I drew my finger across my lips like a zipper.

"What?" he repeated.

I maintained silence.

"Okay. Okay." He held his hands up in surrender.

I pretended to unzip my lips. "Okay what?"

He shook his head slowly. "You aren't snoopy."

"Are your fingers crossed?"

"Oh, for Pete's—"

I drew the lip zipper closed.

"No, my fingers aren't crossed."

"We saw Olive, the manager, sneaking out of Sarge's place." I told him how she had parked across the highway and taken a back way out of the RV park to get to her car.

"And I suppose you're going to blow her little rendezvous all out of proportion? Leave it be, Mattie. Let the woman have a little self-respect." Mo pulled out a bag of pretzels and tore them open. "She's having a fling and doesn't want all the looky-loos gossiping about her."

"You're probably right, but—"

"But nothing. Give it a rest. Just because you got lucky and helped solve a case back home doesn't give you license to get involved down here."

"Lucky, my eye. The sheriff's department would still be trying to solve that case if it weren't for me," I said.

"Right." He angled the bag toward me. "You want a pretzel?"

I pushed the bag aside. "No, I don't want your silly pretzels. I want you to take this investigation seriously. I want you to take me seriously."

Mo sat up and swung his legs around. "Mattie, I am taking this seriously. You forget I have years of experience in law enforcement. I will not worry until there's a need to worry. And you need to stop the Nancy Drew. Okay?" Mo reached over and jiggled my knee. "Hon, this is going to be okay. You don't need to run around trying to prove my innocence."

"But—"

"No buts. Let the sheriff's department do their job. I'm keeping my eyes open. Don't you worry about that. Now can we enjoy our pool time?"

"What do you mean you're keeping your eyes open?"

"Mattie, stop." Mo leaned back on the chaise and slid his hat down over his eyes.

He promptly dozed off. "Crazy old fool. You're going to burn like a charcoal briquette in this blistering sun. And don't even think I'm going to rub aloe on you when you look like a lobster."

What did he mean, he was keeping his eyes open? Was he investigating this on his own? Maybe instead of fishing, Mo was doing his own snooping. That would be just like him. He seemed way too relaxed. But then Mo never was one to let anything ruffle his feathers.

I couldn't wait to call Lizbeth and run this by her. She'd know what to do. But I knew the minute I called, Mo would wake up.

CHAPTER THIRTEEN

When Mo woke, redder than he had been and irritated at me for not waking him, we came home where he promptly brought out the aloe. I felt sorry for him and gave in. Afterward, I made sandwiches for lunch and a watermelon salad for the fish fry. I also threw together a strawberry shortcake dessert that Lizbeth and I had perfected last summer. Mo took a new fishing magazine he'd been wanting to read and went out to the patio. He sat right outside the door, so I didn't want to call Lizbeth and risk getting interrupted. Instead, I sat and made a list of everything I wanted to tell her. If I didn't, I'd forget something for sure.

When Mo saw Stan puttering around at the grill, we loaded our cooler and headed over. While the guys set up the grill, Sandi and I put the finishing touches on the side dishes.

"I went out on a limb and invited Olive and Sarge to join us," I said while tearing lettuce for a salad.

Sandi's eyebrows shot up. "Jeez, you didn't tell them what we saw this morning, did you?" She sliced jewel red tomatoes she'd picked up at the flea market.

"Of course not. I didn't invite them as a couple."

"Thank goodness." She sagged against the counter. "Girl,

for a minute I didn't think I was going to be able to trust you."

I tossed thin slices of red onion, green olives, and chopped pimentos into the salad. "I told both of them they could bring someone."

"How did that go?"

"They both declined, and Sarge hit on me."

Sandi blew out a breath. "Meh! He always talks up the ladies. Don't get your panties all in a twist thinking he's making a pass at you."

My ego deflated quicker than a cold balloon. I waved a dismissive hand in the air. "Ha! Never gave it a second thought."

"Do you think they'll show up?" Sandi arranged the tomato slices on a platter then sliced the cucumbers.

"No. Neither one acted like they had any interest in being social."

"It would definitely be a first for Sarge. Olive comes to yoga, and she'll come when we have bingo or a card game at the rec center. She organizes a monthly trip up to the casino. That woman loves to gamble."

Stan opened the door and stuck his head in. "We've got company."

"Okay, I'll bring some drinks," Sandi said. Before the words were out of her mouth, he'd shut the door. "I invited Kat too. That's probably—whoa! Look at this." Sandi slid the curtain away from the window and moved so I could see.

Olive and Sarge stood on the patio. I did a double take. "Are they together?"

"I'd say so. They're holding hands." Sandi opened the fridge and pulled out the beer she'd been chilling. "Stan has a cooler outside. Let's take these and see if anyone would prefer tea or a soft drink. Grab that bowl of chips, will you?"

"Can do. Well, that solves one mystery anyway."

"Just makes for another mystery," she said. "Why now?

There have always been rumors about Sarge and a mystery woman. So, why did he choose now to come out in the open?" Sandi picked up the bowl and opened the door.

Kat had also joined the party.

"Hey everyone," Sandi said. "Glad you could make it."

Olive's cheeks turned pink. "I hope you don't mind that we showed up."

"The more the merrier," Stan said.

I introduced Sarge to Mo. "I assume you know everyone else," I said to Sarge.

He nodded and took the bottle Mo offered.

Sarge leaned in and whispered, "Hope you didn't take offense to what I said earlier. I was kidding with you. I know better than to crack an offensive joke. That's not who I am."

"I didn't think a thing of it." The less production I made, the better. If the guy really was trying to apologize, then all the better.

He winked and said, "Good."

Mo stepped next to me. "I'm going to steal this guy to help with the frying. You ever fried catfish on an outdoor grill before?" He directed his question at Sarge.

"Can't say I have, but I'll try anything once. Let me at those fish." He followed Mo to the grill where Stan dropped fillets into the oil-filled, cast-iron pot he had placed on the hot coals.

Kat seated herself at the picnic table across from Olive. Sandi took drink orders and passed around drinks to the ladies. Iced tea for me and her and beers for Olive and Kat.

Olive looked over at Sarge and then back at us. "Guess I got some explaining to do."

All three of us talked at once.

"Ya think?" Sandi said.

"Sure do," Kat said.

"No explanation necessary," I said.

"But first, I have to ask about Max because I had several complaints from residents about a dog howling," Olive said.

My ears perked. "Where? When?"

"A couple of residents stopped by. End of your street and the end of the next street over." Olive pointed a manicured finger in the general direction.

"I never heard a dog howling. Did either of you?" I directed my questions to Kat and Sandi.

They both shook their heads.

"My first thought was maybe he'd gotten trapped under someone's RV." Olive took a sip of her beer and paused. "Maybe Mo could check it out after we leave. I sure don't want any more complaints."

I had walked every street in the area numerous times and never heard a dog howling, but then I'd not been listening for a howling dog. "It's worth a look. If you get more complaints, let me know. Maybe we can pinpoint where it's coming from."

"Now tell us about you and Sarge," Sandi said.

"We've kind of been seeing one another," Olive said.

"You could have fooled us," Sandi said. "You did fool us. We had no idea." She gave me the side-eye.

Olive ducked her head. "There's a reason we've been quiet."

"Let me guess," Kat said. "Cal?"

Olive nodded.

Sandi frowned. "For real?"

"She was so possessive of him." Olive picked at a flake of dried paint on the table.

"Ha! Not to speak ill of the dead, but she was possessive of anyone who wore pants. Including my Stan," Sandi said.

Olive shrugged. "True."

Sandi scoffed. "I don't worry about Stan. But I never trusted Cal for a hot minute."

Several thoughts aligned and pinged in my brain. But the

biggie was, with Cal not around, Sarge and Olive were free to take their relationship public.

"Why did Sarge still take Cal to dinner once a week? How were you okay with that, knowing how she was?" Sandi asked.

Kat twisted the top off another beer and leaned in.

Olive sighed. "He tried several times to put an end to it, and she'd show up at his place ready to go every time. He said talking to her was impossible. And he didn't want drama. What could I do? I was miserable every time they went, but if she had known about us, can you imagine the scene she would have made?"

"Well, looks like you landed right in the middle of motive land," Kat remarked.

"What do you mean by that?" Olive asked.

Kat leaned back and crossed her arms across her ample chest. "You said it yourself. The only reason you've kept your relationship a secret is because of Cal. Cal's dead, and look who comes parading out in the open. Looks like as good a motive as any."

"Wow," Olive said. "I never thought about that. Jeez, you all don't think I had anything to do with her death, do you?"

I thought about seeing Sarge, all dressed in black, jogging the night of Cal's death. Was that a coincidence?

"We got fish coming up," Mo hollered. "You ladies ready?"

Sandi stood. "I still have a few things to bring out."

"I'll help." Kat slid off the picnic bench.

I was halfway out of my seat when Olive asked me a question. Sandi threw me a glance, and I shrugged.

"We got this," Sandi said. "Stay here."

Kat followed her inside.

"I'm really sorry about being so evasive this morning when you invited me," Olive said.

"Don't give it a second thought."

"Sarge and I had agreed we'd keep our relationship quiet, but then this morning he did the unexpected." She fished a delicate chain from inside the neck of her T-shirt. At the end was a gigantic diamond solitaire engagement ring.

"Congratulations. That's beautiful," I said. "Why aren't you wearing it?"

Olive sighed. "I just don't feel right. Apparently, Sarge had been planning this for weeks. Today is the anniversary of our first date, and he was so excited about popping the question, but when Cal died . . ."

I held a hand up. "Olive, you don't have to explain."

"Will you—" She looked at the RV. "Will you not say anything to the others just yet? I still don't feel comfortable making an announcement, but I wanted you to know the full story since we kind of crashed the party after turning you down."

Ugh, I hated keeping secrets. "I won't bring it up, but if it gets out somehow and Kat or Sandi ask me if I know, I won't lie to them."

"Fair enough." She tucked the ring back inside her shirt.

Stan yelled at the open window. "What's taking so long in there? We got a pile of fish and a group of hungry campers."

Sandi and Kat emerged carrying trays heavy with food while I struggled with the burden of the secret Olive had dumped on me.

CHAPTER FOURTEEN

It was almost ten by the time Mo and I returned home. I told him about what Olive had said about the complaint she'd received about a howling dog.

He blew out a breath. "It's a howling dog, hon. We don't know it's Max. Someone probably has a dog with separation anxiety, and it shows its displeasure at being left alone by howling."

"Or it could be Max. Maybe someone found him and decided to keep him, and that's him showing his displeasure at being dognapped," I shot back.

"Dognapped? Now you're being a drama queen."

Before my mouth spewed words I would regret, I slammed the containers I'd brought home from Sandi's into the sink, turned the water on, and turned my back on Mo. Then I counted to ten. Then twenty. Out loud. Part of me wanted to tell him about the ransom note, but I'd set my mind to see this through. If Mo wasn't going to take trying to clear his name seriously, what hope did I have that he'd take a dognapping seriously. Besides, he'd already scoffed at the idea that Max could have been dognapped. Drama queen! I'd show him.

"Okay, I'll go door to door tomorrow if you want. Will that make you happy?"

"What will make me happy is for you to take this seriously. If he's not back by Friday, what's your plan? Because I'm not leaving without him."

Mo put his arms around me. "I promise we won't leave here without him."

"Good. That's what I wanted to hear." I pulled back and squirted soap into the sink.

"I'm beat. Leave this mess for morning, and I'll help you clean up." Mo yawned and stretched his arms like a gigantic bear getting ready for hibernation.

"No way. There are leftovers to put away and a few dishes. It won't take me long." I gave him a gentle shove. "You go on to bed. I'll have this done before you even start snoring." Truth was, the sooner he fell asleep, the sooner I could call Lizbeth.

"I don't snore." Mo kissed me on the forehead.

"You can't hear it because you're already asleep. Now, go before I change my mind and put you to work." *Just kidding. Go to bed.*

"Okay." Mo shuffled into the bedroom, pretending to snore in an obnoxious tone.

"Pull the door closed. I don't want to hear that racket." *And Lizbeth and I can talk without you hearing.*

In less than ten minutes, I had the leftovers in the fridge and the kitchen spotless.

Before firing up my laptop, I checked at the bedroom door to make sure I heard snoring. After a quick text to confirm she was still awake, I settled on the sofa with my laptop and my best friend.

"How are things in RV land? You solved the murder yet?" Lizbeth laughed.

I leaned in close to my laptop and whispered, "No, but I

think the killer took Max. I got a ransom note warning me not to talk."

Lizbeth's eyes widened. "Are you kidding?"

"Nope." I went on to tell her about my trip to the old barn and the complaints Olive had received about a dog howling.

"You ever heard him howl?" Lizbeth asked.

"No, but that doesn't mean it wasn't him. He's scared. He's in a strange place. He's missing me and Mo." Kind of sounded like me. Only I was missing my best friend and now my dog. I'd howl, too, if it wouldn't wake Mo.

"What are you doing about it?"

"I'm going to find my dog and the killer," I said. "No one is going to get away with taking Max."

"I wish I were there to help."

"Me too. Sandi, the gal next door, is okay. But she's not you. And I still don't trust her." I took a sip of tea, knowing I'd pay for it when I made umpteen trips to the bathroom during the night.

Lizbeth made a pouty face. "You better not replace me."

"She's a seven-day friend. Once we leave here, I'll never see her again. You got nothing to worry about. But I have to tell you, she's nervy. We went on a spy mission this morning. Remember me telling you about Sarge, the guy who sold me that stupid knife?" I recounted how we'd seen Olive sneaking out his back door. "She had parked across the highway, real stealthy like."

"A love triangle." Lizbeth rubbed her hands together. "This is getting good."

"They came to the fish fry tonight—together. And they're engaged." I felt safe confiding in Lizbeth. If I parsed Olive's request correctly, when she'd asked me not to tell the others, by others, I took her to mean all those present at the fish fry.

"Whoa!" Lizbeth said. "Wasn't he involved with the dead woman?"

"Kind of." I explained what Olive had said about how

pushy Cal was when it came to Sarge. "It puts them high on my suspect list, though I want to believe Olive is too kind to do something like that."

"Besides Sarge and Olive, you got any other good suspects?" Lizbeth asked.

"Cal's sister, Ruby, is a mess. I don't know anything about her, but I sure want to talk to her. The two seem to have a love-hate relationship."

"Like me and my cousin. That woman, I swear." Lizbeth and her cousin had a long-standing feud over their grandfather's estate.

"Yeah, I don't know what theirs is all about. Men, probably. I'm still not sure about Sandi. I like her, but she and Cal had a huge dustup at the flea market, and Cal has a history of flirting with Stan. That's Sandi's husband. He could be a suspect too."

"Especially if he had a fling. Maybe Cal threatened to expose a tawdry affair." Lizbeth cackled.

"I think Stan is pretty hen-pecked. But who knows? There's also this gal, Kat. She is a no-nonsense throwback hippie. I don't know about her and Cal. Other than there's no love lost between the two of them. She's had a run-in or two with Cal about the flea market. All of them except Ruby had an opportunity to take Mo's knife from the picnic table. I guess she could have snuck over at night and took it, since he probably left it out there. If Sarge is not telling the truth about it being one of a kind, then Sarge could be a suspect too."

"I think you have to treat them all as suspects," Lizbeth said. "No one gets a pass."

I reached around the couch and pulled out my bag of flea market treasures. "Let's change the subject. This is too depressing."

"I could tell you about the new owners of the Double L Café. They opened back up today, and Donny and I went there for breakfast."

The Double L used to belong to my late mother and more recently my stepfather, Lazy Lou. He'd sold the Double L to Mezo, his best friend and lead cook at the café. Then Lou passed away in December. Mezo sold the café, claiming he didn't have the heart to run it without Lou at the helm.

"No, that's depressing. I can't imagine anyone but my mom or Lou running the place." I fastened the bracelet I'd brought for Lizbeth's birthday to my wrist and wiggled my arm in front of my laptop's camera. "You like?"

Lizbeth's face took over the whole screen as she leaned closer to get a better look. "That's gorgeous. But you know you'll never wear it."

"You're right. I won't, but you will. I was going to wait until we come home to show you, but I couldn't. When I saw it, I knew it was perfect for you." I could save the purse and still surprise her with it.

"I love it. Those colors are perfect for a top I bought. Where did you get it?"

"At the flea market," I said.

"Be careful. I don't mean to pooh-pooh on your parade, but some of that stuff is as fake as can be. They'll insist you've got a rare stone, and it winds up being some kind of resin they poured into a mold in their basement or something," Lizbeth said.

"I'm not worried. These are sea glass. Sandi designs them —not in her basement, but in her RV—and each one is prettier than the next. Her prices are reasonable too." I twisted the bracelet around, admiring how the light from my reading lamp made the glass glow.

"Just making sure. You really have to watch it," Lizbeth said.

"I know. I know. It's disappointing. There's not as many booths as I'd hoped. You can tell it used to be brimming with activity, but so many have closed. Sandi says it's because Cal berates all the booth owners."

"Another reason to keep your new friend on the suspect list," Lizbeth said.

"Jealousy does not become you. I'm going back Wednesday to look for something for my girls." I tucked the bracelet back in the bag and slid it behind the sofa. "I bought a knife similar to Mo's for Michael, but now I'm having second thoughts about giving it to him."

"Remember to haggle like I showed you. Don't let them get away with full price. Except, if you know they're selling the real deal like that Sandi." Lizbeth raised a glass to her lips.

I laughed and raised my glass too. "We'll both be up all night."

"It will give me something to do. The way Donny snores, I'll be awake trying to ignore his snoring. Might as well have something to do other than lie there and decide if tonight's the night I put a pillow over his head."

"I hear you on that. And I can hear Mo snoring from the next room. Max snores too. It's aggravating, but I sure do miss that crazy dog."

"He'll be back," Lizbeth said.

Max was a stray that had been hanging around our neighborhood in Pine Grove. When Mo had a run-in with a suspect, Max had tried to protect him. Mo wound up with a broken shoulder, and Max found a new home with us.

"He's such a great dog. Mo and I are lucky. He rarely barks, has had no accidents in the RV, and he's protective. He'll give one or two little warning growls, but he's not aggressive. All the things you'd want in a dog. Except the snoring, but I put up with Mo. Max's snoring doesn't seem so bad now. I'd give anything to see his wizened old face and hear that window-rattling snore."

I saw Donny, wearing only his boxers, walk behind Lizbeth. "You better tell him I can see him."

"O-M-G! Donny!" Lizbeth's face disappeared and my

screen went gray. "You big goof. I'm on a video chat with Mattie."

"Hey, Mattie," Donny called.

"Love the buffalo-checked boxers, Donny," I said.

"Oh, for pity's sake, get yourself on the other side of the table so I can take my finger off this camera hole. Mattie doesn't want to see you strutting around in your tacky undies."

I laughed. "Too late."

"I got more clothes on than most of those kids at the mall with their pants down to their knees," Donny said.

"Scram!" Lizbeth's face reappeared. I saw Donny tug at the waistband of his boxers in a teasing way.

Lizbeth giggled. "Stop it. Go back to bed."

Donny disappeared, but the boxers sailed across the room and landed on Lizbeth's shoulder.

"I swear on all that is holy, that man is going to be the death of me."

"Sounds like he's getting frisky. You better get off of here." I chuckled, but only because Mo would do the same thing and think nothing of it.

Lizbeth smirked. "I'll show him frisky. Catch you later. Let me know what's going on."

I clicked off and closed my laptop.

CHAPTER FIFTEEN

"You want to go into town for breakfast?" Mo came out of the shower with a towel wrapped around his waist.

"Now you ask me. I just ate cereal and a banana." I rinsed the bowl and put it in the drainer to dry.

"Rats! I was looking forward to biscuits and gravy. Stan goes there every morning. Thought you'd want to tag along."

"And hear fish tales about the one that got away? No, thank you. You go ahead. Though, I don't know how you can be so calm about all this," I said.

"About all what?" Mo poured himself a cup of coffee and headed back to the bedroom.

I followed. "This investigation and Max. It's not like you. I can't believe you aren't down at that sheriff's department right in the thick of things. And you are going to check out what Olive said about the howling dog, right?"

"Mattie, first off, you're the one who begged me to retire. Second, even if I were still working, this is not my investigation. It's not even my town. I trust Sheriff Nevins to do his job." He rummaged through a drawer looking for clean clothes. "I'm heading out to look for Max before I go to the café."

"You're the bottom three drawers," I said. "I took the top three. Everything else is in the closet. It wouldn't hurt to go down and talk to the sheriff and see what they've found. For all you know, Stan might be guilty, and then you'd be guilty by association—hanging out with him fishing and chowing down on biscuits and gravy like nothing happened."

Mo raised his hands in exasperation, which was the wrong thing to do, because his towel slid down. He scrambled to pick it up. "Now look what you made me do. I swear, Mattie, why are you so obsessed?"

"Me, obsessed? I just think you'd want to clear your name is all. It was your knife they found in the poor woman."

"The knife you bought me, I might remind you." He pulled a pair of boxers from the bottom drawer and stepped into them.

"Don't remind me. Why did I even go to the flea market? I'm still not convinced that knife is one of a kind." I turned and headed into the kitchen. "Wednesday, I'm going back over there to look at Sarge's knives again."

"Mattie!" He stomped down the hall behind me.

"What?"

"Leave it alone. I don't want you getting involved." He had pulled on a pair of shorts and was tugging a T-shirt over his head.

"Who, me? I'm not getting involved."

"Listen to me. You can't go around like some amateur sleuth. You got lucky last time. Next time you might not be so lucky."

"Go eat breakfast with Stan and don't you worry yourself about what I'm doing. Text me after you check with the RVs who heard the dog howling." Under my breath, I muttered, "Someone in this family has to take charge."

～

After Mo left, Sandi came over to remind me about yoga.

"We're still having it?" I asked.

"Yeah, apparently Ruby is already up there. I ran to the office to see if Olive had any bug spray, and she told me she'd seen Ruby headed over to the rec center with her yoga mat."

"Great! Give me five minutes to change." I raced inside, pulled on my yoga pants, and switched shoes.

"Can you believe she's doing this class?" Sandi said on the way to yoga.

"I know. You'd think she'd have family coming in. Or that she'd be going home to family. Instead of hanging around here."

"That's the thing. Cal has no family that I know of. Just a string of ex-husbands. I remember telling her about my grandkids one time. She scoffed and said she never had kids, so she didn't have to worry about them bringing around their squalling brats." Sandi frowned. "Shut me up really quick. There's nothing I like more than talking about my grandkids."

"Me too. I only have one, Ben. He's the best baby. My girls, Carrie and Sadie, don't live close, so we don't see them nearly enough." I opened the door, and we walked in.

Several women had already arrived and set their mats out. I grabbed one from the pile by the door, and we found places near the back of the room next to Olive and Kat.

"Hey ladies," I said.

"Quiet down," Ruby admonished. "You're late, and we're centering."

"Well, excuse us all to heck," Sandi said.

Olive shot her a look that said, "Shut up and go with the flow."

I sat on my mat, crossed my legs, and took a deep breath. When I opened my eyes, Ruby had already moved to another position. This time standing on her right leg, the left leg bent, and with her foot resting on her right knee.

I rolled over on my mat and struggled to a standing position. My knees creaked in protest. I had barely gotten to my feet when Ruby dropped to the floor on both knees and leaned forward, touching the mat with her forearms.

The rest of the class was still centering. I nudged Sandi. She opened her eyes and stared at Ruby.

"Aren't you supposed to be calling the moves so we can follow along?" Sandi asked. Her voice reverberated in the room's stillness.

No answer.

The rest of the class struggled to their knees and waited for a response. Ruby drew in a ragged breath and the sobs came. Long, loud, and heartbreaking.

"What the freaking what?" Kat said.

The rest of the women stared in disbelief.

Olive looked around, bewildered. "What should I do?" she mouthed.

Sandi gave her a gentle push. "Go talk to her. We'll gather our stuff and leave."

"Me? Why me?" Olive whimpered.

"Because you own the place. You've known her longer than anyone here," Sandi said. "Go on."

"Yeah," a woman near the door said. "That's what you get paid the big bucks for."

"Let's give them some privacy," Sandi said. "We can go for a walk."

While the other women rolled up their mats, Kat, Sandi, and I lingered.

Olive took a few halting steps.

"Go on," Sandi prodded. "You got this."

Ruby continued to sob, pounding the mat with her fists. Sandi, Kat, and I backed out of the room with Sandi motioning Olive forward. When Olive was next to Ruby, she looked to Sandi for guidance.

"Rip the bandage off," Sandi said from the doorway.

Olive's big blue eyes were as round as donuts. She bent down and patted Ruby on the back. "Shh. Shh."

Ruby shot off the floor like she was spring-loaded—a feat I would have never dreamed possible for someone her age. And a feat that would surely put me in traction. She wiped her eyes, rolled up her yoga mat, and stalked across the floor, leaving a stunned Olive staring after her.

When Ruby got to the door, she said, "What are you gawking at? Get a life." She squared her shoulders, pushed past us, and kept walking.

"Well, all righty then. I guess we've been told to mind our own business," Kat said.

Olive joined us. "Lord have mercy. I tried. Not sure what else we can do."

Sandi piped in. "Guess it's not the right time to ask about funeral arrangements."

"What are we going to do about that?" Olive asked. "Do you suppose Ruby is making those decisions or what?"

"Ladies, I know I'm the newcomer here and really have no say in the matter. I didn't even know Cal, but I'd say to leave it alone. If Ruby wants to share the details, she will. But for now, I think she needs time to process this whole thing," I said.

"Let her stew," Kat said. "No one really gives a rip."

CHAPTER SIXTEEN

"Let's skip the walk, okay?" I asked Sandi on the way back home.

"Sure, what have you got planned for the day?" Sandi hiked her bag higher on her shoulder.

"I don't know. Mo invited me to breakfast this morning, and I brushed him off to come to yoga. Now I'm kind of regretting it."

"Never turn down breakfast at the café," Sandi said. "Have you eaten there yet? The boys have probably already left and headed down to the lake."

"Mo took the Jeep this morning. I was hoping to talk to the owner."

A twinkle glinted in Sandi's eyes. "Oh, are you up to what I think you're up to? Our car is still here. Stan rode with Mo this morning."

"Do you know Olive's daughter's name?" I asked.

"It's Becky or Betsy—something like that. Throw your bag inside and let's go," Sandi said. "I'll go get my keys and check on Scooter."

I ran in, changed clothes, and was back in Sandi's car in less than ten minutes.

~

Sandi pulled into the lot of the Sunflower Café and parked next to our Jeep. "Looks like the boys are still here," she said.

"This is going to be more difficult than I thought. Play it cool and don't say a word to Mo. He's been on my case about this and told me to stay out of it," I said.

Sandi cut the engine and opened her door. "Same here. Stan will blow a gasket if he knows what I'm doing. He says I'm too nosy for my own good."

I followed Sandi and the aroma of bacon to the door. As she reached for the handle, it opened. Stan, Mo, and to our surprise, Sarge walked out.

Mo's face brightened. "Hi, hon, thought you were going to yoga."

"Ruby had a meltdown, and Olive canceled yoga," I said.

"Looks like Olive needs to get a new yoga instructor, what with Cal gone and all. Ruby's surely not going to hang around the RV park after all this." Stan threw his arm around Sandi and hugged her. "I expect she'll be moving on."

"We could get so lucky," Sarge muttered. "I don't expect she'll be going anywhere."

"Since we can't exercise, we're going to try out those biscuits and gravy you've been bragging about," I said to Mo.

"Darn, we were just leaving. We could hang around a bit and have coffee with you," Mo said.

I waved a hand. "No need. I'm sure you boys got plenty of fish to catch today."

Stan cuffed Mo on the shoulder. "We can grab breakfast with the gals another day."

Mo winced and rubbed his shoulder. It was the same shoulder he'd broken at Christmas when he'd tumbled off a loading dock while in pursuit of a killer. Actually, he hadn't tumbled. Max, a stray back then, had pushed Mo out of harm's way. Dog and man had been best buddies since.

"That settles it," I said. "We'll do breakfast together another day. What did you find out about the howling dog?"

Mo's shoulders drooped. "I talked to several people on both streets and nothing. No howling last night. Though, one guy thought we'd gotten Max back. He said he saw someone late last night walking a dog that looked similar to Max. Said he'd seen the flyers we've put up and swore it was him."

"That's curious," I said.

"Not really. It was dark. Probably just another black dog," Mo said.

"You're right." I didn't think he was, but I didn't want to arouse his suspicions. If someone had Max, they'd need to let him out once in a while to do his business. And what better time than after dark or before sunrise. "Go catch some fish."

"Whew!" Sandi said after the boys had jumped in the Jeep and fired it up. "That was a close one."

The Sunflower Café was a cozy little establishment. Shiny yellow booths lined two outside walls. An enormous stone fireplace took up the third. Tables covered in cheerful sunflower tablecloths filled in the center area, and twelve swiveling chrome-and-yellow stools lined the front of a gleaming counter. Sunflower-themed quilts hung from the exposed rafters overhead. The floor was a checkerboard of yellow and white tiles.

"Oh, this place is so sweet, it almost makes my teeth hurt," I said.

Sandi laughed. "Yeah, the owner is almost as sweet. She's a transplant from Alabama. She oozes southern charm and can also sling an insult with the best of them. You never know you've been cut off at the knees. There she is now." Sandi waved.

A woman with bright red hair, teased and twirled into a gigantic beehive, headed our way.

"Hey darlin', haven't seen you in ages. Who's your friend?" The woman wore a sunny yellow dress with a swirly skirt, a starched white apron, and a name tag pinned to her ample bosom that read "Birdie."

"Birdie, this is Mattie. She belongs to the good-looking stud who was here with Stan and Sarge. Mattie, this is Birdie, the diner owner."

Birdie fanned her face with an order pad. "Now that was a fine-lookin' hunk of man if I say so myself."

I gulped and cut a glance to Sandi. The last thing I needed was another Cal.

Birdie guffawed and tapped my hand with her pencil. "Just joshin' ya, honey. I got me more man than I can deal with." She pointed to a window that opened into the kitchen.

An aging Elvis look-alike deposited a plate on the window counter and yelled, "Order up."

"That's my Lawton. Isn't he about the most handsome devil you ever laid eyes on?" She placed a hand under her chin and blinked several times.

"Um, sure. He's quite the looker," I said.

"Y'all go find yourself a spot. I'll bring over the coffee pot straightaway." She made a shooing motion.

"Could I have an iced tea, please?" I asked.

She had already started back behind the counter.

"Hey, Birdie, make her tea unsweet!" Sandi yelled. To me, she said, "You think this place makes your teeth hurt from sweetness, you haven't tasted her sweet tea."

"I hadn't even thought about it. In Missouri, tea is tea," I said.

Sandi dropped into a booth and pulled out a menu and handed it to me. "Already know what I want."

"Let me guess. Biscuits and gravy?" I opened the menu and scanned the offerings.

"Everything here is good, but you haven't eaten a biscuit until you've had one of Lawton's. They're so light, they'll float right off your plate unless you drown them in his heavenly gravy."

Birdie returned with two coffees and an iced tea.

"Biscuits and gravy times two," I said.

Birdie stuck her thumb and forefinger in her mouth and whistled. Her husband's face appeared in the serving window. She held up two fingers, and he nodded.

"Scooch over, baby," she said to Sandi. "I need to get off my dogs for a bit while it's slow. Dang, this getting old ain't for sissies, is it?"

Sandi and I nodded in commiseration.

"Terrible thing, what happened to Cal," Birdie said. "They got any idea who did it? Tried to get some gossip from y'all's menfolk, but their lips were clamped tighter than a tick on a hound dog."

She leaned across the table and whispered, "I heard from another source that the knife that was used to kill her belonged to a temporary at the RV park."

I felt my face flush. Sandi choked and spit coffee on the table.

Birdie clamped a hand over her mouth. "Lawdy mercy, oh no. Me and my big mouth. Not your big old hunk of handsome. I don't for a second believe that."

"No, Mo didn't do it, but it was a knife just like one I bought at the flea market. One that Sarge claimed was one of a kind." I knew I was treading on thin ice. I was the newbie here. Sarge and all the permanent residents had a history with Birdie and this town, so I had to watch how I broached the subject of Olive's daughter and her schedule. The last thing I wanted was Birdie running off to Olive and telling her I'd made an accusation.

Birdie patted my hand. "Course not, doll. I could tell he was an upstanding, fine gentleman."

"He's a retired chief of police," I said proudly.

"Did Olive's daughter work Friday night?" Sandi blurted.

I wanted to crawl under the table. My mouth dropped open, and I was at a loss for words.

Sandi patted my arm. "No worries. Birdie's a straight shooter. She'll tell it like it is."

"What? Y'all think old Goody Two-Shoes might be responsible for Cal's death?" Birdie smacked the wad of gum she had in her mouth then roared with laughter. "That'll be the day that Ms. Sunday School goes to the dark side."

"Oh, you don't know nothin', girl," Sandi said, her voice beginning to match Birdie's southern drawl. "We caught Olive doing the walk of shame Sunday morning."

Birdie's long eyelashes flew open and her eyes rounded. "No way. I believe you're pulling my leg. That woman does not know the meaning of"—Birdie clamped her hand over her mouth and looked around the restaurant—"s-e-x."

Sandi drew an X across her chest. "Cross my heart."

Birdie let out a whoop. "Sky's going to fall in for sure. Who's the lucky man?"

"Oh, please. I'm not giving it up that easy," Sandi teased.

Birdie clapped her hands and twisted in her seat like a ten-year-old getting a new bike. "Come on. You can't let me hang. You know I love me a juicy piece of gossip."

"Yes, I do, but first, focus. Tell me if her kid worked Friday night," Sandi insisted.

I kicked her under the table and gave her the stink-eye.

Sandi waved nonchalantly. "It's not a big deal. Birdie loves good gossip. Besides, she's in an excellent position to hear stuff."

"Truth," Birdie said. "People pay no attention to what they're saying around here. It's like I'm wearing an invisible cloak. They're more worried about what the next table's going to hear. I can flitter from table to table and the conversation never stops. As long as I don't act like I'm eavesdropping, people keep yapping. Now quit holding out on me."

"First, tell me about Olive's daughter. Did she work Friday night?"

"Yes. She pulled a double shift. We were slammed, and I

had a server call in sick, so I called Becki in at six Friday evening, and she worked until six Saturday morning," Birdie said.

"Any chance she left early?" Sandi asked.

"Absolutely not. She was the only server. My night cook is a cantankerous old goat. He would have blown a gasket. I'd have gotten a phone call and a chewing out if she had taken as much as an extended potty break, much less left. He doesn't put up with any nonsense. That's why I keep him around."

Birdie's husband brought out a heaping platter of golden-brown biscuits, and two bowls filled to the rim with creamy gravy speckled with pepper and loaded with chunks of sausage. He slid an empty plate in front of Sandi and me. "Enjoy, ladies. If you need more biscuits or sop, let me know."

"Sop?" I questioned.

Birdie cackled. "That's what he calls his gravy. You sop it up with the biscuit. Now spill."

While I tore apart two biscuits and covered them with sop, Sandi repeated our tale about Olive's early morning retreat from Sarge's place.

"For land's sake. Don't that beat all you ever stepped in? Miss Goody Two-Shoes sharing the sheets with Sarge." She fanned her face with both hands. "Now that man is hot with a capital *H*." She stopped abruptly, and her brows scrunched together. "Wait, you think Olive punched Cal's ticket over Sarge? This is just too good to be true."

"We don't know who did," Sandi said. "But you have to admit, with Olive and Sarge being an item, and Cal acting like a heifer in heat every time Sarge shows her the least bit of attention, the thought has crossed my mind."

I laid my fork down. "But, if Olive babysits, and her daughter worked a double shift that night, that rules her out, right?"

Birdie frowned. "Darn! I never thought about that. Olive

would never leave those youngins alone, and Becki was here all night. So, who's next on our list?"

Sandi leaned back. "Our list?"

"Yeah. I told you, I get all the good gossip in here. You tell me who your suspects are, and I'll keep my ears open. But I got to know who to pay attention to, you know. Can't just be eavesdropping on everyone," Birdie said.

"Makes sense." I shoved another forkful in my mouth and considered my suspects. Sandi and Stan were still on my list, but I couldn't divulge that to Birdie. She'd blabber to Sandi.

"Sarge, for sure," Sandi offered. "Then Ruby. She and Cal might be sisters, but there's no love lost between the two of them."

"Yeah, Ruby might have been making a play for Sarge," Birdie said.

The door opened and two couples walked in.

"Birdie," Lawton hollered, "you got customers."

Birdie slid out of the booth. "Okay, who else?"

"Kat. Do you know her?" I asked.

She nodded. "The hippie-looking woman? I do. Not well. When she's here, she usually shows up for Tuesday Taco Night. Don't know much about her. She's not very talkative."

Lawton ambled over to our table and swatted Birdie on the backside. "Come on, baby. Quit your gabbing. I gave your customers water, but from the looks of it, they're ready to order."

Birdie gave him a light punch in the shoulder. "Like it'd kill you to take an order once in a while?"

Lawton held up his hands as he continued to the kitchen. "Woman, these are cooking hands. They got skills beyond order-taking. Get your *tuchus* in gear and get me some orders. Idle hands, you know."

"Okay, gals. I gotta skedaddle. I'll keep my ears open." Birdie waved at the new arrivals. "Hey, folks."

"She's a bundle of energy," I said.

"Yeah, I love her to pieces, but I can only take small doses of her." Sandi took a mouthful of biscuit and gravy and moaned.

"Why's she so anti-Olive?"

"From what I gather, Birdie and Lawton have been wanting to get into the food truck business. Their original idea was to park one at the flea market. Olive turned them down flat. Wouldn't even listen to their idea, much less consider it. Birdie's made several pitches for how a food truck would be a good thing to draw more customers," Sandi said. "Lawton even tried a time or two, and every time, Olive rejected them. Last time she accused Lawton of trying to seduce her. Birdie flat-out blew a gasket. The two have been mortal enemies ever since. Olive told both of them to stay away from the flea market."

"Jeez. How does that work with Olive's daughter working here? Must be difficult for her." I pushed my plate away before I gorged myself.

"Nah. The daughter is sweet as Birdie's iced tea. Everyone loves her. She's a single mom, struggling to pay her bills and stay afloat. Her husband died in Iraq or Afghanistan or one of those places while serving our country. He was a hometown boy—football hero. Birdie would eat glass before she'd turn on the girl." Sandi chuckled. "Unfortunately, that courtesy does not extend to Olive."

I thought about what Birdie had told us. "If Becki worked a double shift, that leaves Olive off the hook as a suspect, right? Would she go off and leave the kids alone?"

Two cops walked in and sat in the booth behind me. Birdie followed with two cups and a pot of coffee.

Sandi wiped her plate with the last morsel of biscuit. She shook her head then, when she'd finished chewing, said, "No way. They're just babies, two and four. Olive would never leave those two alone for a second. She's devoted to those kids. Why, if anything happened to those little ones, she'd never forgive herself."

Another couple came through the door, followed by two young women with four children lagging behind. The women headed to the booth behind Sandi, dragging high chairs and booster seats with them.

"It's fixing to get noisy. Let's pay up and get out of here," Sandi said.

CHAPTER SEVENTEEN

After Sandi dropped me off, I took another walk through the RV park, calling for Max and listening intently for any sign of a dog barking or howling. When I turned down Cal's street, I saw her front door standing open. The crime scene tape dangled from the wrought-iron porch posts.

"What are you gawking at?"

I jerked so fast, pain seared through my neck. Ruby stood on the porch, hands on her hips and a dishcloth slung over her shoulder.

"Sorry. I was shocked to see the door open. Is everything okay?" I asked.

"My sister's dead, and I gotta clean out all her junk. No, I'd say everything is not okay." Her belligerent tone belied the tears welling in her eyes.

Despite my misgivings and Ruby's lack of friendliness, I found words coming out of my mouth that I never expected to mutter. "You need help?" I walked to the porch and stopped short of the front step.

Ruby shrugged and went inside. It wasn't a yes, but it wasn't a no. She scared the bejesus out of me. Her blatant hostility wasn't something I encountered often in my hometown of Pine Grove. Before he had his morning coffee, Mo was about the grouchiest person in town. Once he had a generous amount of caffeine, he tamed down nicely. Needless to say, I always had the coffee pot set to turn on thirty minutes before we woke up.

I'm going to do this if it kills me. On second thought, it might. I drew together all my courage, opened the door, and stepped across the threshold.

Boxes lined the sofa and the end tables. White trash bags lay in various stages of fullness in the center of the floor.

"Why are you in such a hurry to get this place cleaned out?" I asked.

"End of the month is coming up, and Olive wants her rent." Ruby threw a pile of magazines into one of the trash bags.

"I'm sure if you talked to her, she'd understand," I said.

Ruby whipped a paper from her pocket, unfolded it, and shoved it at me. "Yeah, you'd think so. But Miss Queen Bee wants her rent. She's been itching to get Cal and me both out of here. She might have had her wish with Cal, but she'll play heck getting rid of me."

I read the letter, not believing the sternness of the wording. Basically, Olive told Ruby she had until the end of the month to either pay up the next month's rent or vacate. If either of those situations did not occur, Olive would change the locks and seize the property.

"I'm not a lawyer, but I don't think she can do this without a court order or something." Mo had executed plenty of eviction notices during his tenure as chief of police.

Ruby smirked and hiked a shoulder.

"I'm sure she can't," Ruby agreed, "but I'm not in any mood to fight, and I don't want to get dragged through court. It's not like this place is worth fighting for, and I don't need it. Cal didn't have a lot, but she has a few antiques that belonged to our mother and grandmother. I don't want those going into storage and me getting stuck with a bill until a court settles it."

"Makes sense. I didn't take Olive for being such a stickler," I said. "That letter was pretty blunt."

Ruby wagged a hand dismissively. "Form letter. She gets a lot of deadbeats in the short-term rentals. Rumors are going around that she's in financial trouble. You've seen how ratty this place is. Getting worse every day." She tossed another pile of magazines into a trash bag.

I stared at the room. "What can I do to help?"

"If you want to finish here, I'll take the bedroom. Figured I'd box Cal's clothes and drop them off at one of the churches in town. Or not." She laughed a half-hearted laugh. "Maybe they're better suited for a resale shop. I can't see a clothes pantry being all gung-ho to pass out Cal's clothing."

"Probably a good idea." I had only seen Cal once or twice, but I couldn't even imagine church ladies digging through a rack of Cal's clothing without blushing.

"If it's disposable, toss it in the trash. I've gathered all the antiques. Box the rest of the stuff, and I'll drop it at the resale shop. If you can't decide, set it aside and I'll look at it." She grabbed a handful of trash bags and started down the hallway. When she was almost out of sight, she turned. "Thanks."

I cleared a bookshelf, cleaned off the end tables, and taped and labeled three boxes. After I plucked two wall hangings from the wall, I leaned them against the sofa, unsure whether they belonged to Cal or stayed with the unit.

Ruby made a trip through to collect my trash bags. She carried a purse similar to the ones I'd purchased at the flea market. "You got any need for a new purse?"

I shivered and shook my head. "No thanks." The thought of using a dead woman's purse gave me the creeps.

Ruby pulled the flap open. "She never used it. It still has the paper inside."

"I bought one just like it at the flea market," I said.

Ruby set the purse on an end table. "Guess I could give it back to Kat. Cal made her life miserable about the dang thing."

"How so?"

"It's no secret that Cal harassed everyone at the flea market. She got crazy because Olive wasn't picky about what people sold. If they could pay the booth fee, Olive let them in. Cal claimed it took away from the value of the goods we all sold. If Cal could intimidate the booth owner to close, she did. That's part of the reason Olive's in financial trouble. Not long ago, the lot overflowed with booths. Cal and Olive have been at odds for years. Every year more and more booths shut down because of Cal's ranting."

"I heard her arguing with Sandi about jewelry," I said.

"Yeah, she and Sandi were like a chem lab experiment gone wrong. Sandi sells classy stuff she designs. The stuff Cal sells is junk with the price marked up. Sandi consistently outsells her. Cal's tried her intimidation tactics several times, but Sandi ignores her."

"What was her beef with Kat?" I asked.

"Who knows? This is only Kat's first year with a booth. She's been coming down for years, but she's never had a booth before. She was an easy target. Or so Cal thought. Kat didn't back down either. It's usually the first-timers Cal runs off, but Kat's been around her enough, she just dug her heels in."

"If you don't want the purse, I'll take it back to her," I said. That would be a good excuse to talk to Kat and find out more about her relationship with Cal.

"Fine by me. I'll throw these bags in the golf cart and take them up to the trash bins. Will you be okay while I'm gone?"

I nodded.

"Will you clean out the cabinets and fridge?" She grabbed the bags I had tied up and pushed her way out the door.

I grabbed several empty boxes from the stack, emptied the

cabinets, and made a pile of open items on the table for Ruby to take. By the time she returned, I had worked up a sweat.

"Why don't you knock off for now?" Ruby said. "It's getting ready to storm, and you're going to get soaked if you don't leave soon. I can handle the rest."

"Jeez, I didn't even notice. I wondered why it was getting so dark." I taped a box and stacked it near the door. "This is all ready. You want me to come back tomorrow?"

"No, I got a handle on it," Ruby said. Then she did something that floored me. She hugged me, an unexpected hug filled with emotion. "Thank you for helping."

"It . . . It was nothing," I stuttered, still reeling from a hug from the woman who had been so belligerent and standoffish. "I don't mind at all. No one should have to do this alone."

She shrugged, despite tears welling in her eyes. I returned the hug. She clung on and let the tears fall. We stood like that for what seemed like forever.

After a sharp crack of thunder, Ruby pulled away.

"Sorry," she said, wiping her eyes. "What's wrong with me? I'm not a crier."

"You've lost your sister." I patted her arm. "Totally understandable. If you need someone to talk to, you know where I am."

"You know, Cal and I were close once, best friends." Ruby wiped her eyes and sniffled. "As we got older, we changed. Maybe desperation from getting old and being alone. I guess more than one family has split apart because of stubbornness. We didn't appreciate what we had in one another."

Another crack of thunder rattled the windows.

"You better go," Ruby said. "The sky is fixing to open up, and the only thing I have to give you to keep you dry is a trash bag." She shoved one into my hand. "Now go, before the downpour starts."

CHAPTER EIGHTEEN

I barely made it in the door before the rain fell. Huge drops pelted the RV. I was watching out the window when Mo pulled up in the Jeep. When he didn't come in, I realized he was waiting for the rain to slow. My phone dinged with a text message.

MO: IF IT DOESN'T SLOW DOWN SOON, I'M GOING TO MAKE A RUN FOR IT.

ME: I'LL OPEN THE DOOR WHEN I SEE YOU COMING. THERE'S AN UMBRELLA UNDER THE SEAT.

The old fool wouldn't take the umbrella. He'd make a mad dash and get himself soaked. I went to the bathroom and grabbed a towel. By the time I returned, his lack of patience had gotten the better of him. He splashed across the patio and up the steps.

I held the door open, and he sprinted in, dripping rainwater everywhere. He grabbed the towel I held and scrubbed his head, then patted himself to soak up the water.

When he had dried off and changed clothes, he sat at the table with a cup of hot tea.

"I did something interesting today," I said.

He poured an abundance of sugar into his cup and sat back. "Something tells me I'm not going to like this."

"There you go. You always think the worst. Do you want me to tell you or not?"

"Fire away."

"I helped Ruby clean out Cal's belongings." I took my cup to the table and joined him.

"That's the sister, right?"

"The first time I met her, she was intimidating, but today she seemed nice. Not sure why she puts on such a hard front," I said.

Mo scrunched his eyebrows. "Why was she in such a hurry?"

I told him about Olive's letter.

"Makes sense if the crime scene has been released." Mo's left eyebrow lifted. "You were in there snooping, weren't you?"

Dang! Why didn't I think of that? It was the perfect opportunity, and I blew it. "No, smarty-pants. I was not."

"Regardless, leave it alone." Mo lifted his cup. "Wanna sit outside?"

"In the rain? Are you nuts?"

Mo glanced out the window. "It's barely drizzling now. I'll open the awning."

"Nah, I think I'll call Lizbeth. You go ahead. I'll come out when we're done," I said.

"Ha! That'll be the day. Once you fill her in on everything you've been doing that you won't tell me, then she'll have to tell you all the juicy stuff going on in Pine Grove, like how many days the neighbors left their trash can at the curb after trash day. Or who did or didn't go to church last Sunday. Or who saw whose husband flirting with somebody at bingo."

I threw a napkin at him. "Go on outside with yourself and quit making fun of us. I miss her."

Mo retraced his steps and planted a kiss on my forehead.

"I know you do. I miss Donny too. Just because we're traveling doesn't mean we set aside those friendships. They'll always be our friends. But we can make new ones too. Take Stan, for instance. He's an all right guy. And you like his wife okay. That Sarge guy is a decent fellow too. No telling how many new people we'll meet on this journey. As long as—"

"I know. I know. As long as I have the internet, we'll always be in touch with Lizbeth and Donny. It's not the same, but you're right. Now take your tea bag out before it gets too strong."

∼

Mo left the next morning long before I rolled out of bed. He'd stuck a note to the bathroom mirror saying he'd left the Jeep for me and would try to be back by noon. After walking down to the rec center with Sandi for yoga and finding a canceled note, Sandi and I parted ways. Her daughter was bringing the kids down for a morning of swimming. With Sandi busy, I wanted to talk to Birdie—alone.

I finished my chores in record time and grabbed my purse and keys. It had been twenty-four hours since we'd seen Birdie, and I was curious if she had heard anything related to Cal's case.

I had turned the key in the ignition when Sandi tapped on the window, causing me to jump.

"Where you headed?" she asked through the glass.

I put down the window and killed the engine. "To the café."

"You want company? I could eat my weight in biscuits and gravy today," she said with a sullen tone. "Jenny called. One of the kids has a slight fever. They're staying home."

She looked so dejected; I couldn't tell her no. I had felt the crushing blow many times when the weather had turned nasty, and one or both of my girls had to cancel a trip home. It was a horrible feeling and even more heart-wrenching when grandchildren were involved.

"Hop in," I said.

When we were seated at a booth in the Sunflower Café, Birdie waved, grabbed an iced tea and two coffees, and beat a path to our table.

"Hey, chickees." She dropped into the booth next to Sandi and hugged her.

"Olive canceled yoga this morning," Sandi said. "After Ruby's meltdown yesterday, I guess she didn't want to take a chance of another session going off the rails."

"That and the fact that Olive sent her a notice to clean Cal's place out by the end of the month." I removed the lemon slice from the rim of my glass and squeezed it into my tea.

"What? No way," Birdie said. "Well, if that isn't mean and vindictive, I don't know what is."

"Hold on, gals. Don't be so quick to judge. Olive needs the park to make money. Every vacant unit and RV pad is costing her money," Sandi said. "Every week we have more booths sitting empty."

"Okay, I get that, but if Miss Fancy Pants is hurting for money so badly, she could let me and Lawton put our food truck out there. She's just being a snot."

"I can't comment since I don't know the entire story," I said, proud of myself for staying above the fray. If I'd learned one thing about small-town living, it was that you didn't wade in between two bickering women. Eventually they would sort things out or not, but either way it wasn't my business to take sides.

"Phooey. Let's not talk about that. It sets my blood to boiling. I don't need my blood pressure shooting through the roof," Birdie said.

"You heard any good gossip?" I wasn't about to let our

conversation take another sidetrack before I found out what she knew.

Birdie wrinkled her nose. "Maybe. Maybe not. I don't know if it's important."

"Spill," Sandi said. "Let us be the judge."

Birdie leaned in real close. "After y'all left yesterday, two gals came in. I've seen them around before, but they ain't locals. I figured they're staying at the park over by y'all because they were driving a golf cart."

"A golf cart?" I prodded. "They drove down the highway in a golf cart? That's craziness."

"There's a trail from the back of the RV park that cuts through the woods. It's a pretty far piece for people to walk it, but golf carts take that way all the time. Anyway, they were talking about how the flea market is a rip-off. They also mentioned being swindled big time, and the one was surprised the law hadn't shut the place down."

"Was she talking about any booth in particular?" I asked.

"That's the thing," Birdie said. "I might have gotten a touch too involved in eavesdropping. They clamped their lips together when they saw me."

"We're looking for a toy hauler then," Sandi said.

"A toy what?" I asked.

"It's a towable RV with a drop-down ramp. Lets you drive your big kid toys right up inside a special storage section. People with golf carts, dune buggies, ATVs, and motorcycles use them because they can't tow those behind the RV like we do our cars," Sandi said.

I shook my head. Would I ever learn all this camping lingo? "I'll take your word for it."

"Hey, what y'all want for breakfast? We're getting so swept up in talking, we're forgetting the important stuff. Lawton made cinnamon rolls, and they are to die for." Birdie swiped across her forehead with the back of her arm, making a fainting motion.

"Not for me. Mo is going to have to widen the front door if I keep eating the way I am." I puffed out my cheeks.

"Lawton'll cut that thing in half. Only eat half the calories that way." Birdie was already heading to the kitchen.

I sighed.

Sandi jostled my arm. "Lawton doesn't make them often. If you miss them today, you won't get another chance before you leave. Come on, we can be good tomorrow. Boiled eggs and dry wheat toast. Yum."

Before I could answer, Birdie set down three small plates. "I had him cut it in thirds. I'll share the guilt with y'all."

My third, heaped with creamy icing, hung over the edge of the small plate. Sandi was already digging in, so what choice did I have?

I cut into mine, and the warm fragrance of cinnamon made my mouth water. Before I allowed myself to speculate how many calories the roll contained, I shoved a piece in my mouth, and I was hooked.

The next several minutes we filled with oohs and ahs as we enjoyed the cinnamony goodness. I finally pushed my plate aside. "I can't eat another bite."

"Tell me you're not leaving that morsel." Sandi forked the last of my roll and shoved it into her mouth. "Mmm-mm. Tell me that wasn't the best cinnamon roll you've ever eaten."

I nodded my concurrence.

"Your hubby thought so too," Birdie said.

Sandi groaned. "Stan said he was going back on his diet."

Birdie stacked up our plates and pushed them to the edge of the table. "Not Stan. He just got a coffee to go."

"And Mo stayed to eat a cinnamon roll? That's odd."

Lawton arrived with fresh tea for me and topped off Sandie's and Birdie's coffees.

Birdie patted him on the butt. "Thanks, honey bear."

"Wonder what they're up to." Sandi stirred a packet of sugar into her coffee.

"Sheriff Nevins cornered Mattie's husband, and they got to talking. So, Stan took his coffee to go, and Sheriff Nevins invited Mo to stay and have a cinnamon roll. On him, if you can believe that. Guess your hubby isn't a suspect anymore. Never knew that cheapskate Nevins to buy anyone breakfast, much less a suspect in a murder investigation." Birdie blushed. "Not that I think your husband had anything to do with Cal's death. I'm just saying it was unusual."

Sandi cut me a glance. "How bizarre. Guess Stan didn't want to be a fifth wheel."

I looked around the café. "If Stan left, where's Mo?"

"That's the even weirder part," Birdie said. "After they finished their rolls, he left with the sheriff."

She could have slapped me with one of Lawton's frying pans, and I wouldn't have been more shocked. "Left? What do you mean left? If they were eating breakfast together, it had to be friendly. Who eats breakfast with a suspect and then hauls him off to jail?"

Sandi set her coffee cup down. "Columbo, that's who."

My left eyelid twitched. "What?"

"Columbo always makes the bad guy feel like he's off the hook and then BAM!" She pounded the table for effect. "Then at the last minute, he turns around with his cocky grin and lowers the boom."

"Listen to yourself. This is not television." My insides roiled with fear. Could that be the case? Had the sheriff hauled Mo off to jail after filling him with cinnamon rolls and coffee?

"Stop it." Birdie held her hands in the air, signaling an intervention. "That's not what happened. Listen to you two. They had a friendly breakfast. At least they were laughing and cutting up like old pals. When they walked out the door, I ran to the window and looked. Mo got in the front seat. Now I ask you, if the sheriff were arresting your husband, wouldn't he handcuff him and toss him in the back? There's no way Nevins is letting him in the front. Your husband's a retired lawman. Nevins would have frisked him to make sure he wasn't packing heat."

My shoulders relaxed, and I let out the breath I'd been holding. "You're right. And Mo does still carry his service revolver. The city gifted it to him when he retired."

"See, nothing to worry about." Birdie slid out of the booth and picked up our plates. "My word. I can't believe I forgot to tell y'all what Becki said."

"What?" Sandi asked.

"Y'all were right about Olive and Sarge. Becki spilled the beans this morning. On the nights Becki works, Sarge has been parking his slippers under Olive's bed."

"Parking his slippers?" I asked.

Sandi nudged my arm and winked several times. "That's code for doing the nasty."

"Oh." I pressed my hand to my mouth in surprise.

"Yesterday I came in early and let Becki go home an hour before her shift ended." Birdie shifted her weight and set the plates back on the table. "She said Sarge was sitting at the breakfast table in his skivvies when she walked in. I'd have paid money to see that."

CHAPTER NINETEEN

"You know what that means?" I said as we drove around the park looking for toy haulers.

"What?"

"We've been dismissing Olive because she'd never leave her grandkids alone."

A grin sprouted on Sandi's face. "She's back on the list. Right? If Sarge was there, Olive could have left the kids and not felt the least bit guilty. If Sarge sleeps anything like Stan, he'd never be the wiser."

I flicked a thumb in the air. "Exactly. Now, how do we tell these toy thingamabobs from any other RV?"

"Look for big doors that open on one end," Sandi said.

I hunched over the steering wheel, staring at the RVs as we inched down each street. It was difficult because of the way the owners had parked. The ramp doors were in the rear, and all the units were backed into their spots. Eventually, Sandi identified five toy haulers. We ruled out four of them by chatting up the owners, pretending that our husbands were interested in buying toy haulers, and we were seeking firsthand experience to help them decide.

Blah. Blah. Blah. Never had I ever been so sick of hearing someone extolling the virtues of anything.

"It's a dream on wheels."

"I can fit everything inside except the kitchen sink. Wait, I do have a kitchen sink. Ha! Ha!"

"My wife told me it was the RV or her. Now she's my ex." *Hardy-har-har*.

Two of the units belonged to ATV owners. And the other two carried a variety of kayaks and canoes for the lake. All owned by knuckleheads.

The fifth unit occupied a space at the end of the next street over. We figured we'd hit the jackpot when we saw a pink golf cart sitting next to the RV. Unfortunately, no one answered our knock.

"Keep an eye out for that pink golf cart. If you see someone driving it, that's who you need to talk to," Sandi said. "I'll be working my booth in the morning. I'll watch at the flea market, but I can't get away until after we close at noon."

"Will do." I pulled the Jeep into the spot next to my RV and cut the engine. A piece of paper stuck to the RV door fluttered in the breeze.

Stan drove in seconds after we'd gotten out of the car. To my surprise, Mo was with him. I decided to let this play out and see if Mo would tell me what had transpired. Saying goodbye to Sandi and waving to Mo, I hurried to the door to retrieve the paper. I crumpled the note and stuffed it in my pocket, hoping Mo hadn't seen it.

Mo walked by and pecked me on the cheek. "I'm going to take a shower and change into something that doesn't smell fishy."

"Something smells fishy all right, and it's not your clothing," I said when he was out of earshot. While he showered, I flattened out the wrinkled paper. Another black-and-white image of Max took up the bottom of the note. A bone and a rubber ball sat off to the side next to a dish. Max still wore the glum expression he'd had in the previous image. This time the photo was zoomed out, and I saw the unmistakable carpeting that screamed *RV*. No one in their right mind would have that in their home.

THE DOG IS ENJOYING HIS NEW HOME. IF YOU KEEP YOUR MOUTH SHUT, YOU WILL GET HIM BACK. IF YOU DON'T, HE'LL BE COMING HOME WITH ME WHEN I LEAVE.

I folded the note and took it to the bedroom where I hid it in the drawer with my bras. Mo would never in a thousand years look there. Several things came to mind. I never saw the face of the person at Cal's place, so I couldn't identify them even if I wanted to. More importantly, they saw me and thought I could. Also, Sandi and I were together when the note writer stuck this one on my door. Stan and Mo were together, except for the time while Mo and Sheriff Nevins were eating cinnamon rolls. Did that clear Sandi? I wanted to think it did, but Stan was a question mark. Stan had no way of knowing Mo would strike up a conversation with Sheriff Nevins, but did he take the opportunity to come back here? Could they be hiding Max in their RV? Only one way to find out.

I slipped into my sandals, went to their RV, and pounded on the door. My knock was met with ear-splitting growling and barking, but not the thunderous sound of Max's bark.

Sandi opened the door with Scooter in her arms. He still growled and snarled like he wanted a piece of me. "Hey, what's up?"

"Uh . . . Uh . . ." I stuttered.

"Is everything okay?" Sandi clamped her hand around Scooter's muzzle for a moment. "Shh! It's Mattie."

"Uh, yeah. Sugar. I need to borrow sugar." Seriously, I wanted to smack my forehead. Of all the cliché things to ask for.

"Come on in." Scooter had finally calmed down. Sandi set him on the floor, and he rushed over and sniffed my leg.

A rush of tears filled my eyes. I swiped them away before bending down to pet him. I wanted so badly to find Max, but relief washed over me that he wasn't at Sandi and Stan's. I realized that I didn't want Sandi to be guilty. I liked her, really liked her. It would have been devastating to find out that she had not only kidnapped my dog but also murdered Cal. My emotions so overwhelmed me that when she came back with a zippered bag of sugar, I threw my arms around her and hugged her while tears streamed down my face.

She pulled back and stared. "Are you okay? You're acting a little weird."

I realized how stupid I looked and shook my head. "I'm fine. Seeing Scooter made me sad, and I realized how thankful I am to have you as a friend."

She smiled. "Me too. I'm glad we met."

I turned and started out the door.

"You forgot your sugar." Sandi handed me the bag over my shoulder.

I set the sugar on the picnic table and took a short walk down our street and up the next one. Nothing had changed at the RV with the pink golf cart. By the time I returned, Mo had emerged from the shower.

"How was your day?" I asked.

"Good. Good. How about yours?"

I moved closer. "Just. Dandy." I pinched my words, enunciating each one. "Anything interesting going on?"

He toweled off and pulled on a pair of boxers followed by a pair of shorts. "Nope. Same old. Same old."

"Nothing?" I took a step forward, closing the gap between us.

He shook his head and tugged on a T-shirt. "No."

"You sure you want to go with that?" I tilted my head and gave him the death stare. If that didn't break him, nothing would.

He pulled me into a hug.

"What are you doing?" I twisted away. "Don't even think about distracting me."

"I don't know what's going on in that head of yours. I'm going to make a glass of tea. You want one?" Mo stepped past me and headed to the kitchen.

"Don't even try to change the subject." I followed him.

"I'll take that as a no on the tea."

"You're not going to tell me about your rendezvous with the sheriff?" I grabbed a glass from the dish drainer and poured my own tea. I'd show him.

Mo took a deep breath. "How'd you know about that?"

"I eat cinnamon rolls, too, you know."

Mo sat at the table and patted the bench next to him.

I reluctantly slid in. "This better be good."

"Sometimes a cinnamon roll is just a cinnamon roll."

I snorted. "And sometimes it's not. What gives?"

"Trust me, Mattie. The less you know, the better."

"Where have I heard that before? Oh wait, I know. You used to say those exact words when you were working an especially dangerous case. Well, guess what, Mo Modesky. You're retired."

He ignored me.

"You *are* retired, aren't you? The city council appointed your replacement."

Mo sighed. "Yes, I retired from Pine Grove."

"You're mincing your words. What aren't you telling me?"

When he didn't reply, I knew what was going on. "We didn't come to this RV park because the fishing was good, did we? There are a dozen other parks in the area, and you didn't randomly choose this down-on-its-luck one, did you?"

"No."

"You and Sheriff Nevins cooked this whole thing up, didn't you?"

Mo turned to face me. "Mattie, Nevins and I go way back. He knew I was retiring. When he found out we were going to be RVing, he called and asked for my help."

"Mo Modesky! And you didn't tell me?"

"I couldn't. I can't take a chance on you blowing my cover."

If steam could have rolled out of my ears, it would have. Mo didn't push my buttons often, but when he did, it was usually something to do with his work and him treating me like a helpless airhead. "Blowing your cover. You sound like some shady private investigator."

He gulped, and the tips of his ears reddened.

"Is Stan in on this?"

"No."

"Oh. My. Word. Are you investigating them? Did you buddy up to Stan becau—wait. Is this about Cal's death?" My left eye twitched. "I don't understand. Cal died after we got here and with your knife. Or a knife that looked like yours. I'm so confused."

"Honestly, the less you know, the better." He took both my hands in his. "Promise me, you will not say a word to Stan's wife. No one. Not Olive or Sarge. No one."

"Now you have me worried. Are they suspects?"

"Everyone is a suspect," Mo said.

"Great. How can I even talk to Sandi without thinking you're investigating her?"

"It's going to be hard, but I know you can do it. With that said, Stan invited us over for another fish fry tomorrow. You think you can whip up something to go along with the fish?"

"Are you serious? How can we even be around them?"

"No choice. I can't act any differently than I've been

acting. Besides, I really do like the guy. But I can't blow my cover. And you can't blow it for me. Understand?"

"What about me? Sandi was with me at the café this morning when Birdie spilled the beans about you having breakfast with the sheriff. She's going to be asking questions." I had basically ruled out Sandi, but I couldn't tell Mo. Doing so would confirm his suspicions that I was still snooping. Not only did I have to figure out who had Max, but now I had to know what Mo was working on.

"She and Stan are heading up to their daughter's house for the afternoon. Something about one of their grandkids. Tomorrow she'll be working at the flea market."

"Oh, no. She said one of the kids was sick. I hope it's not bad." At least I could buy some time. I didn't know if I could keep my mouth shut much longer. Thank goodness for Lizbeth. I never kept anything from her, regardless of what Mo said.

"I don't think so. Stan didn't seem worried. He said they'd be back tonight. We're going out on the boat again tomorrow." Mo tipped his glass and drained the iced tea. "You can handle this, right?"

"I'm still not happy you lied to me about why we came here."

"It might be splitting hairs, but I didn't technically lie." He quirked an eyebrow and winked. His silly wink usually made me giggle. It didn't this time.

"Split it however you want." I crossed my arms over my chest.

"I did it for your own good."

"Still not working."

Mo winked again.

"Stop it." I wanted to stay mad, but I knew I wouldn't. Mo would never do anything to hurt our relationship. And it wasn't like I hadn't bent the truth with him once in a while with stuff I didn't want him worrying about.

"Truce?" He wiggled his eyebrows and made kissing noises.

I sighed, knowing he'd worn me down. "Truce. I still don't understand about this morning. You left here with Stan. But you had breakfast with Nevins by yourself and still went fishing with Stan."

"Stan and I stopped by the café for coffee. Nevins was there for breakfast. We got to talking. I told Stan that we'd gone to the academy together, so Stan invited him to go on the boat. Nevins had ordered breakfast, so Stan said he'd go gas up the boat and give us time to catch up. No big mystery."

A thought crossed my mind. "How long did you and Nevins sit there talking?"

Mo shrugged. "Ten minutes, tops. We wanted to get out on the lake. Stan had barely finished gassing the boat and getting the gear ready. What does it matter?"

"Just thought it was rude for you to ignore Stan like that." Ha! Quick thinking. Okay, so maybe Stan didn't have time to come back here and leave me a note. The dock was in the opposite direction of the RV park.

"It wasn't like that. They knew each other from Stan coming down. It was Stan's idea to give us some time to catch up. The boat needed gas. Don't make a big deal out of it."

"Men! Now you want me to sit through a fish fry and act like everything is hunky-dory. Ugh."

"That's exactly why I didn't tell you in the first place. Now can you do this or not?" Mo asked.

"I might have to have a migraine."

"Fine." Mo nudged me to let him up. "You can stay here. I'll make an excuse for you. But don't be surprised if Stan's wife doesn't come banging on the door to check on you."

I slid off the bench and let him out. "I'll go."

He took our glasses to the sink. "Thanks, hon. It won't be

bad, I promise. It's just a fish fry. Not an inquisition. You ladies do your thing. Us guys will do ours."

I didn't tell him my thing was me and Sandi investigating Cal's murder. Sandi and I wouldn't be talking about it tonight or in the morning. I needed to avoid her until the fish fry tomorrow evening. Once we were around Olive and Kat, Sandi knew not to bring up Cal's murder. It was the in-between time that worried me.

CHAPTER TWENTY

Later that afternoon, the text alert sounded on my phone.

LIZBETH: YOU HAVE TIME TO CHAT?

ME: IN FIVE MINUTES. PUTTING A PIE IN THE OVEN.

LIZBETH: YOU GOT IT.

I slid the pie into the oven, made myself an iced tea, and fired up my laptop.

"Hey," Lizbeth said when our video chat connected. "You look like I could reach out and touch you. I'm so glad we can do this."

I agreed. We spent the next thirty minutes gossiping about all the news back home. Lizbeth had her finger on the pulse of Pine Grove and relayed all the juicy tidbits. She let me know that the young couple we rented our house to had been busy keeping my flower gardens pretty. The young man had even been working on a rose bush I had given up on.

"What's going on down there?" she asked when she'd run out of updates.

"Hold on." I peeked out the window to check on Mo. He was dozing in a lawn chair. "You won't believe this." I recounted my conversation between Mo and me, knowing full well Lizbeth would understand, commiserate, and assure me I wasn't wrong to be miffed. Back home, we constantly compared our husbands' shortfalls, each one trying to outdo the other.

Lizbeth's mouth opened and closed in shock. "I. Can't. Even. Are you okay with it? Is this a one-time thing, or is he going to be doing detective work as a retirement gig?"

I shrugged. "I'm more upset that he didn't tell me. And it's not like I tell him everything. The law is in Mo's blood. How can I be mad at that?"

"You can always be mad." Lizbeth chuckled. "We're wives. That's our job. We have to keep them on their toes. I can find twenty-seven reasons a day to be mad at Donny. Has Mo put a crimp in your investigation?"

"Of course. He told me I can't say a word to Sandi or any of the other women. Yet we have to go to a fish fry with them tomorrow night. Lucky for me Sandi is busy this afternoon and tomorrow morning. I just have to figure out a way to stay away from her until the fish fry. That won't be easy." The oven timer dinged. "Hang on a sec. I have to take my pie out of the oven."

I removed the pie to a cooling rack and checked on Mo. His chair was empty. He'd probably made another trip around the park looking for Max.

"Mo is on the loose," I said when I came back to my laptop. "If I change the subject quickly, you'll know why."

"Is Mo investigating the murder?" Lizbeth asked.

"Beats me. He's all hush-hush. And the murder didn't happen until we were already here."

"I bet it's all connected." Lizbeth drummed her fingers on the table. "We have to figure out what the connection is."

"Brilliant," I said flippantly. "How in the world do we do that?"

"How about drugs? Maybe there's a drug kingpin in the RV park that Mo is investigating."

I thought about Stan and Sarge and dismissed the idea of

them being kingpins. "Only if they're pushing male enhancement drugs." I laughed. "Seriously, this place is a bunch of old people. No one is coming here to get high. Maybe buying black-market laxatives or acid reflux medicine."

Lizbeth slapped the table, causing her laptop to wiggle. "I got it. I know."

"What do you know?" Donny appeared behind her. "Afternoon, Mattie. What are you two plotting?"

"Scram, Donny," Lizbeth said. "We're plotting to take over the world, and you're interrupting. Go get the mail and make yourself useful."

We waited until Donny left, and Lizbeth had made sure he shut the door.

"I swear, I don't know how you put up with Mo being around all the time. Donny's been home for two days because he has vacation time to burn, and he's driving me up a wall. When he retires, we're going to need a bigger house."

"You'll adapt. Try living in a motor home. Besides, Mo's rarely here," I said. "Now what was your big revelation?"

"Jeez. See what I mean? Now I'm distracted." Lizbeth snapped her fingers. "Oh, I know. I bet it's either stolen goods or counterfeiters. I've been reading up on that since the last time we talked. It's big money, and flea markets are rife with it."

"What kinds of stuff are you talking about?" I asked.

"Anything with a designer logo. Watches, jeans, cosmetics, perfume, jewelry, and handbags to name a few."

I glanced down at the bag that contained the purses I'd bought for me and Lizbeth. Then I remembered I had the one Ruby found at Cal's place that I needed to return to Kat.

The RV door opened, and Mo walked in.

"Got any tea?" Mo asked. "I'm parched."

"Looks like Mo's back. I better let you go," Lizbeth said. "Think about what I told you. It might be worth checking out."

I nodded and ended our call.

"What's worth checking out?" Mo asked, pouring himself a glass of tea.

I kicked the bag of purses farther behind the sofa. "Nothing important. She's been filling me in on the gossip back home. She said the renters have the place looking fantastic."

"And?" He dumped two spoons of sugar into his glass and stirred it.

"And what?" I topped off my tea. "Lots of good gossip."

"That's what worries me," Mo said.

CHAPTER TWENTY-ONE

Mo left early for breakfast with Stan. They had a full morning of fishing planned. At least that was what he said. Sandi had her booth to keep her busy. Since I had the Jeep, I was tempted to take a run past the café to see if Mo was with the sheriff. I shook off the thought and took another stroll around the park looking for Max.

As I made the last turn to head up the main road to our street, the pink golf cart carrying two women raced past me, headed in the direction of the flea market. I made an about-face and followed, albeit at a much slower pace.

Even fewer booths were open today. Only a handful of people shuffled up and down the aisles browsing for bargains. If the booth owners made their rental fee today, they'd be lucky.

I didn't stop to browse as I made my way past the booths. There'd be time for that later. I only cared about finding the pink golf cart and its occupants.

"Hey," Sandi called as I approached. "Did you talk to Mo about his breakfast with the sheriff?"

Why hadn't I avoided this section? "I'll fill you in later.

Have you seen the pink golf cart? It passed me while I was walking."

"No. Was it headed this way?" She craned her neck and looked both ways down the row of booths.

"Yeah. I turned around immediately but lost sight of them. There were two women about our age."

Sandi laughed. "Everyone here is our age. If they park that cart and walk, you'll lose them."

"Then I better quit yakking and get moving."

"Dang!" Sandi sighed. "Wish I didn't have to work. If you catch up to them, stop back and let me know what happens."

I nodded and backed away from the booth, waving. "Catch you later."

I finally spotted the cart a couple of rows over and quickened my pace. When I heard arguing, I halted in front of a vacant booth two spaces from where the women had parked the cart.

The booth next to the kerfuffle was also vacant. I opened the tent flap and slipped inside.

"What's the problem?" I heard a woman say.

"This piece of junk fell apart the first day I used it," another woman shouted. "The stitching disintegrated like it had dry rot. Look at this."

"It looks like you pulled it out to me." This came from the first woman, whose voice sounded like Kat's.

Were they arguing over the designer purses Kat sold? I peeked out of the tent flap and tried to orient myself.

"Give us a refund or we'll report you," said a third woman. "There is no way this stuff is authentic. Probably made in a sweatshop in a third-world country."

I moved closer to peek out of the tent, tripped over the canvas flap, and went down hard on my bad knee. Four curse words came to mind, but I bit my tongue. Instead, a high-pitched screech erupted from my mouth.

When I recovered my senses, three women stared down at me.

"Are you okay?" one of the golf cart women asked. She reached out to offer assistance.

I waved her away. "This will take time, and I don't want to pull you down on top of me."

Kat and the other woman returned to the booth.

I wallowed around in the gravel until I'd gotten my footing and was able to stand. My knee throbbed like the dickens, and I knew before I looked that blood was running down my leg. I took a tentative step and groaned in pain.

"Are you staying in the park?" the woman asked.

I nodded.

"I can give you a lift home."

"You're a lifesaver. I'd call my husband, but he's out on the lake."

"Clare!" she called to the other woman, who was still yelling. "I'll be right back. You hold tough and get our money back. If she gives you any trouble, call the sheriff."

Clare flashed a thumbs-up.

"I'm Lettie." She pulled a package of tissues from a cubbyhole in the dash and handed it to me. "Where to?"

"Thanks. I'm Mattie. Space eighteen—the street before the golf cart crossing in the temporary section." I dabbed at my throbbing knee, stopping to pick out specks of dirt and gravel.

"Fantastic. Clare and I are the next street over. I know right where you're set up." She hit the accelerator and off we went, spewing gravel behind us. "Oops, didn't mean to do that."

"Do you mind if I ask what was happening back there?" I asked.

She took the turn out of the flea market too fast. I grabbed for the dash to steady myself.

"Whoa, Nelly! I'm a little reckless." Lettie eased off the accelerator. "Oh, that woman is a thief—pure and simple. Clare and I bought handbags last Wednesday. Mine fell apart the first time I used it."

"Oh, that's terrible."

Lettie waved a bangled wrist in the air. "You're telling me. I'm reporting her to the manager. If she's a decent manager, she'll close that booth down. I looked up how to spot a fake designer bag on the internet. Those purses are definitely fake. The clasp wasn't even metal. It was plastic, painted to look metal. And leather? Excuse me, but it was fake. That bag was so stiff, if it had gotten cold, it would have cracked. I blame myself for not looking closer. She claimed they were designer. I wanted to believe I was getting a good deal."

"I bought two from her last weekend. Do you suppose they're fake?"

"Absolutely! Girl, go demand your money back before she shuts down her booth and disappears." Lettie made the turn onto my street.

"Will do." The question was how. Kat would be at the fish fry tonight, but that didn't seem like the ideal place to make such a demand.

Lettie pulled in front of the RV. "It was nice meeting you, Mattie. How long are you staying?"

"We leave Friday." At least that was the original plan until Max was dognapped. I unfolded myself from the cart, testing my knee while I put weight on my other foot. "Yikes, that hurts."

"Do you need help?"

"I'm good."

"If you're sure."

I nodded. "I'll be fine."

"Take care of yourself. Hope to see you before you leave. I have to go collect Clare before she kills that woman. Then we're going to talk to the manager." Lettie waved as she drove off.

And just like that, all the thoughts I'd had merged into one cohesive idea.

CHAPTER TWENTY-TWO

All of the stress from the last several days descended on me like a cloak. I had cleaned, bandaged, and iced my knee, trying to ward off the pain. It finally took several aspirin and a nap to calm it down.

I was lying on the couch with a cool cloth on my head when someone knocked on the door, which brought back the dull throb.

"Just a minute." I swung my leg over the side of the couch and took my time standing. Pushing the curtain aside, I saw Olive outside. She gave a tiny wave indicating she had seen me. Why had I looked out the window? I wanted nothing more than to go back to the couch. Now I had to entertain her. I opened the door slowly. "Hi, Olive."

She rushed in, practically knocking me over. "I understand you had an accident at the flea market today."

The breathlessness in her tone stunned me, and it took a moment to digest her words. "What?"

"Lettie Monroe told me you fell at the flea market. I have some forms I need you to sign." She pushed a pile of papers at me.

She could have led with a "What happened?" or "Are you

okay?" but no. Just "Sign these papers." I assumed to release her from any liability.

I stepped back. "Thanks for your concern."

Her face registered shock. "Oh, what's gotten into me? Are you okay?"

"Yes, I banged up my knee. Nothing to get excited about. I got tangled in a tent flap and went down."

She blew out a breath. "It's . . . I can't afford a lawsuit. I have signs posted saying we're not responsible for accidents. I needed to make you aware."

"It's not a problem, Olive. I take responsibility for my own actions." I hobbled over to the table and sat down. "Come on over. Let me see what you have."

Olive handed me the papers and sat down.

I scanned the pages and pages of legal mumbo-jumbo and didn't understand most of it. My head throbbed, breaking my concentration. I shuffled the papers back in order and stacked them on the table. "Can I have Mo look at these? I have a massive headache. Once he does, I'll bring them down to the office."

Her eyebrows shot up. "It's a simple document."

"I know, but I can't think straight." She wasn't going to bully me into signing anything. And if she insisted, I would become more resistant. Two could play her game. I would not be rushed.

She quirked an eyebrow. "What did Lettie tell you?"

That question took me aback. "I beg your pardon."

"I know Lettie is spreading rumors about the flea market. She's a busybody with too much time on her hands. Did she tell you her cockamamie story about counterfeit merchandise?"

"As a matter of fact, she did." I hadn't had a chance to look at the purses I'd bought from Kat thoroughly, and I wasn't about to drag them out and show them to Olive before I talked to Lizbeth.

"She's lying," Olive said. "Between her and Clare, they cause more trouble than anyone here."

"More trouble than Cal and Ruby?" I shot back.

"What's that supposed to mean?"

"Nothing. I just thought Cal and Ruby were the biggest thorns in your side." The minute the words were out of my mouth, a realization hit me full force. Cal had already reported Kat to Olive. Of that I was positive. "Did you know about the counterfeit merchandise before Lettie told you?"

Olive's face turned scarlet. "I . . . I don't know what you're talking about."

"I think Cal told you first, and you turned a deaf ear. You didn't want to risk losing another booth. What I don't know is if she involved the authorities."

"Cal?" Olive stood. "I don't know what you're talking about. Why are you saying these things?"

"I think you do. And I think you knew if it became public knowledge, it would ruin you. The flea market is already suffering, and so is the RV park. With Cal out of the way, you got rid of a major obstacle to rebuilding your business. And your love life." The words spilled out of my mouth. I balled my fists in frustration. Why hadn't she left me alone? Why had she kept pushing me? Mo was due home any minute, and I couldn't wait for him to walk through the door. I envisioned him wrestling her to the ground, handcuffing her, then apologizing to me for not keeping me in the loop. I'd show him.

"Wait!" Olive's shoulders slumped. "Are you accusing me of killing Cal? You can't even believe that. Bouncing back from a few booths closing is one thing. Cal's murder is going to ruin me. My cancellations are piling up since the news got out. My only hope of salvation is if this place would burn to the ground so I could collect the insurance." Olive clamped a hand over her mouth.

My mouth dropped open.

"I didn't mean it like that. Mattie, you have to believe me. I didn't kill Cal. Not that I didn't want to. She was a pain in my butt. Come on, you can't believe I'd kill her."

What am I doing? If Mo were investigating Olive, he would kill me big time. I winced, shocked that I'd let my frustration get the better of me. "No," I said, backing off. "I'm sorry. I don't know what's gotten into me."

"You've been hanging around Sandi too long. She's another gossipmonger. I swear I don't know what it is with all of you. Don't you have anything better to do than spread rumors?" Olive squared her shoulders. "Sign those papers and have them back to me this evening. It's not my fault you're a klutz."

Mo did not come busting through the door. Instead, Olive jerked it open and tromped out, mumbling under her breath.

CHAPTER TWENTY-THREE

When Olive turned the corner and I was certain she was gone, I texted Lizbeth and arranged a quick video chat to fill her in on my conversations with Lettie and Olive. I'd tried before I'd taken my nap, but she was at the salon getting her nails done. Then when she was available, I'd fallen asleep. Despite my headache, I wanted to talk to her before Mo returned.

One of the drawbacks of the RV was not having an office where I could shut the door when I wanted privacy. At home, we had a basement and a garage where Mo hung out and worked on his projects. I had my office/craft room where I quilted or worked on my craft *du jour*. We respected each other's domains. Mo wanted nothing to do with crafting or computer stuff. And I didn't want to get roped into one of his woodworking projects or mowing the lawn.

Lizbeth's face appeared on my screen.

It seemed like forever since I'd seen her in person, though it had only been five days. And in two more days, we'd have this huge behemoth parked in her driveway for a week while Mo swapped fish tales with Donny. And this Cal nightmare would be behind us. I hoped. The only thing missing in that equation was Max.

"What's going on?" Lizbeth asked.

I filled her in on the conversation I'd eavesdropped on at Kat's booth, including my stupidity taking a spill in the gravel.

"Ouch. Did you get ice on your knee?"

"Yup, first thing when I got home, but it still hurts. At least I'm finally getting some relief from the headache."

"Maybe you should have the knee x-rayed."

"If it doesn't get better, I will." I pulled out the bag of purses and spread them on the table. "It embarrasses me to tell you this, but I bought purses from her." I held up all three.

"Good grief. When you go all in, you go all in," Lizbeth said.

"One was for you. But the third one was Cal's. Her sister gave it to me when we were cleaning her place. After I overheard the conversation at the flea market, guess who shows up at my door?"

"Kat?"

"Nope, Olive. Apparently, Lettie, the woman who brought me home, made a beeline to the office to report Kat. She also squealed on me for falling." I went on to explain about the forms Olive brought.

"She's covering her butt. If she's in financial trouble, the last thing she needs is a negligence lawsuit. Who knows? She may not even be paying her liability insurance," Lizbeth said.

"She's paying some of her insurance. She said she'd be better off letting the place burn to the ground and collecting on it than killing Cal to get rid of her."

"Did she really say that? That's all kinds of scary." Lizbeth leaned back in her chair. "Did you accuse her of killing Cal?"

I ducked my head. "Kind of, and she took offense, but I

think she was trying to make a point with her insurance comment. I backed off real quick."

Lizbeth giggled. "Donny, stop it. He's parading around on the other side of the room with just a towel on. Crazy old man. Go get dressed. We're supposed to be going to dinner with the Coopers."

"The Coopers, really?" Wanda Cooper had the biggest mouth in all of Pine Grove. On top of that, she could never get through a meal without sending half her food back to the kitchen and making a scene about it. Lizbeth and I had both experienced Whiny Wanda at various club functions. We'd vowed never to eat in public with her again.

"Don't get me started. It's all Donny's fault. Randall cornered Donny at the hardware store. You know how Donny can't say no. So, now we're having dinner with them." Lizbeth's eyes crossed. "I wish we could call in sick."

I shivered. "Good luck. Let me know how long it takes her to send her plate back. And watch what you say to her or else everyone in town will know before your dessert arrives. She'll be texting all the juicy gossip. Remember, our conversations are sacred."

"That goes without saying, you silly goose."

I trusted Lizbeth with my life, but it never hurt to remind her. We both loved a good rumor now and then, but we'd made a pact never to divulge our conversations.

"What brand are those purses again?" Lizbeth asked. "Let's do some internet research."

I told her the brand and picked up one of the bags. It felt soft and supple, like my favorite purse—one I'd splurged on a couple of months ago. The second bag felt the same way. I wondered if Lettie knew what she was talking about. I looked closer.

"This is bizarre," I said to Lizbeth. "Neither of the bags I bought has a label. Nothing that marks it as designer. I can see where the label has been removed. There's still stitching on the little pocket inside. And the leather feels like the real deal."

"Strange," Lizbeth said. "What about the third bag?"

When I picked up the last one, I instantly felt a difference. This bag was stiff, just like Lettie had said. I unzipped it, and sure enough, the inside pocket contained the designer's label —sewn on crooked. This one was definitely different. Even though they looked alike, that's where the similarities stopped.

"I think I have a fake one and two real ones." I held up the third bag so Lizbeth could see it. "This one feels horrible, and there's a label inside. Only, the label looks wonky."

Lizbeth paid me no mind. She was staring at the screen, and her lips moved, but no words came out.

"Did you hear me?"

"Hold your britches on. I found an interesting article. Check the metal parts and the inside lining."

"Okay." I felt the rings where the handles attached to the bags. The two I'd purchased from Kat were definitely metal. The third felt lighter. I scratched the surface with my finger-nail, and silver paint flaked off, revealing a white plastic ring. I held it close to the camera for Lizbeth to see. "Look at this. It's plastic."

"How about the lining?"

"What am I looking for?" I asked.

"See if you can spot a difference."

I turned all the bags inside out. In my two, the lining fit perfectly and felt like quality material. In the third one, the lining fit poorly, and the seams puckered. "Wow. I don't understand."

"Are you positive the last bag was bought at the flea market?" Lizbeth asked.

"I wouldn't bet my life on it, but Ruby—that's Cal's sister —said it was."

"This article talked about designers who sell last-season

products to distributors. It would explain the two bags you have without labels. Other than looking like a designer bag, there are no identifying marks. Right?"

"Yeah, nothing that says who made these bags. Except the third one has a label."

"Maybe she's selling a combination of fake and last-season designer bags. Probably gets the fake ones cheaper and then blends them in with last-season bags."

"I guess. Do you think it ties into Cal's murder?" I asked.

"The bigger question is, is this what Mo is investigating? If so, you better tread lightly."

I grimaced. "He'd kill me for sure. Then the sheriff would have two homicides on his hands."

"What's your next step?" Lizbeth asked.

"I feel like I need to give Kat the benefit of the doubt. She knows I overheard a portion of her conversation with Lettie and her friend. I'm going to straight-up ask for my money back and show her this purse that Ruby gave me."

"Be careful. Kat might be the murderer, especially if Cal threatened to report her." Lizbeth's face pinched in a frown. "Don't make me worry."

I chuckled. "I could wait to see if she offs Lettie and her friend. They both threatened to report her to the authorities."

"That's not funny."

A knock on the door interrupted us. "You in there, Mattie?"

"O-M-G! Kat's at the door," I said. "What do I do?"

"You can't let her in," Lizbeth said.

"I know you're in there. Olive told me she just came from here." Kat pounded on the door again.

"She knows I'm here," I said. "I could go outside. Surely she won't kill me in broad daylight."

"I have a better idea." Lizbeth told me her plan, and I agreed.

"Coming." I glanced over my shoulder at my laptop before opening the door.

Kat stood there. To say I felt more than a little uneasy was an understatement, but I trusted Lizbeth.

"I need to talk to you about earlier," Kat said.

My knees trembled. I had to get myself under control, or I would foil Lizbeth's plan.

"Excuse me for a minute." I raced into the bedroom and shut the door. I took several deep breaths, willing myself to calm down. Slow and steady, old gal.

When I returned, Kat was inspecting the purses I still had out. I motioned for her to sit at the table. The spot Lizbeth and I had discussed.

Kat didn't budge.

"Make yourself comfortable." I sat down opposite of where I wanted her. "You have to be tired from standing in your booth all day."

She sighed and took the seat. "How's your knee?"

I instinctively flexed my stiffening leg under the table. "It hurt like the devil, but hopefully I didn't do any lasting damage." I hesitated a minute, giving her ample time to proceed with her explanation.

"How much did you hear back there?" Kat continued to stare at the purses.

I opened then closed my mouth, leery of her frankness. "I, uh . . . What do you mean?"

"Were you spying on my conversation with Lettie and Clare?"

"I was walking and tripped," I said.

Kat shifted in her seat and leaned in. "What did Lettie tell you?"

"Why would Lettie tell me anything?" I kept my eyes focused on her.

"Because Lettie has a big mouth, and you were a new audience. She also ran to Olive yapping about something she knows nothing about." Kat jabbed a finger in the air. "And I want to know what she told you."

It was not in my nature to outright lie—maybe little fibs about how Mo's growing bald spot was not noticeable, or how Lizbeth's crow's-feet were more like laugh lines. Or my inevitable trying to dance around the fact that I was investigating a murder and not letting on to my husband that I was in deep.

"She said you all had a disagreement and Clare was handling it." That pretty much summed it up without digging into the details.

"I want to know her exact words." This time she slapped the table to emphasize her point.

I flinched. "Our conversation centered mostly around my knee."

She picked up and inspected the bag Lizbeth and I had determined was fake. The one that came from Cal's place. "Where did you get this?"

A lie caught in the back of my throat, and I pushed it down, letting it evaporate as the truth slid by it. "Ruby gave it to me." I glanced at my laptop positioned oh so carefully behind Kat and saw Lizbeth nodding, urging me on. "I helped her clean out Cal's place, and she gave it to me since she doesn't carry a purse. I was going to give it back to you until I found out it's a fake."

Kat jolted like an electric shock had zapped through her body. "Is Ruby spreading lies too? Or did Lettie tell you that?"

Seeing Lizbeth's face, knowing she had my back, or literally Kat's back, emboldened me. "Lettie told me you sold her a fake one, but I did my homework and read about them on the internet. These two aren't fake, but all the designer labels have been removed." I pointed to the bags I'd purchased.

"You don't know anything. Lettie and Clare are busybodies," Kat insisted.

Kat was making too big a deal out of Lettie and Clare, and it gave me pause. Oh, how I wished I could talk to Lizbeth. Kat being this upset sent my imagination into overdrive. Lettie and Clare made one accusation to Olive, and now Kat was all up in arms. How had she reacted to Cal and her constant needling? Or worse, what had she *done* about Cal's constant needling? She had never been at the top of my suspect list, but she had been here with Olive the night Mo's knife disappeared. I glanced up at Lizbeth and hoped she had my back because I was about to step into the deep end of this mess.

I took a deep breath and summoned my courage. "That's not what I think. You want to know my theory?"

"Go for it, Miss Marple. I can't wait."

"I think Cal was on to you. You were the one I saw running from Cal's house the night she was murdered," I said. "You—" I stopped when I saw Lizbeth pointing frantically to Kat.

"What?" Kat's eyes flashed with a fury that scared me, but Lizbeth's presence gave me strength.

"You stole Mo's knife from the picnic table, and you killed Cal with it, didn't you? And you have Max? Where's my dog?"

Lizbeth smacked her forehead and picked up her phone.

"I did. She wouldn't give me the purse, and she had contacted the authorities. And you couldn't keep your nose out of it. Now you're going to join her in her heavenly repose. And you will never see your dog. Never!" She grabbed a vase of flowers from the table. When she did, Lizbeth screamed, which startled Kat. I screamed too.

Kat grabbed the fake purse, lobbed the vase at me, and ran.

The vase hit the side of my head, and cold water flooded across my face. I crumpled to the floor like I'd been tackled by a linebacker.

CHAPTER TWENTY-FOUR

"Mattie! Mattie!" Lizbeth's voice surrounded me like a warm, fuzzy blanket. "Hon, wake up. Mattie!" Her voice grew more insistent.

I opened one eye and rolled to my side. "What happened?"

"Mattie. Thank goodness. Are you okay?" Lizbeth's face took up the entire screen of my laptop.

I rubbed the side of my head, which was wet. "Am I bleeding?" I struggled to my knees. Pain shot through me.

"Don't try to get up," Lizbeth warned.

"How long was I out?" I crawled to the couch and pulled myself up, cringing each time I put weight on my bad knee.

"Too long. You scared the poo out of me. You went down like a sack of rocks when that vase hit you," Lizbeth said.

"Dang! She got away with the purse, didn't she?" Tears stung my eyes, or maybe it was the nasty flower water. I rubbed my eyes with the tail of my shirt.

"She did."

A car door slammed outside. "Uh-oh, someone's here. You don't think she's coming back, do you?"

"I called Mo when you accused her of killing Cal," Lizbeth said. "It's probably him."

As if on cue, the door swung open and Mo thundered up the steps. He simultaneously scolded and hugged me. Tears filled Lizbeth's eyes, and she swiped them away.

"Aw, don't cry," I said.

"What?" Mo asked.

"Lizbeth's crying," I said, pointing to my laptop.

"What are you talking about?" Mo swiveled his head.

"Lizbeth and I were on video chat when Kat showed up."

"It's a good thing too," Lizbeth said. "If not, she might have killed Mattie."

I gave her the evil eye. "Thanks, traitor."

"I ought to—" Mo pulled me to him and hugged me until I almost couldn't breathe.

"Hey, you're squashing me." I pulled back.

"I'm going to disconnect and leave you two alone," Lizbeth said.

Mo shook his finger at her. "You're not going anywhere. You two have got some ex—"

Lizbeth was gone. Disconnected.

I wished I could disconnect too. Mo couldn't stand tears, and I wasn't one to cry easily. I certainly wasn't one to cry to gain his sympathy or to keep him from being mad at me. Not that I hadn't thought about it once or twice. Instead, I decided to level with him. Lay it all out there. He could like it or lump it. We married for better or worse, so he could deal with it. He had for more than forty years.

"She got away, Mo. Kat's the one who killed Cal. All because she was selling fake designer purses at the flea market." The words tumbled out of my mouth.

"Sheriff Nevins has a warrant for her arrest. She's not going anywhere," Mo said. His tone was stiff and angry. "I swear, Mattie. What did you think you were doing? I told you to stay out of this."

"This?" I rose and grimaced when I let my weight rest on my knee. "This what? Were you investigating Kat? The flea market? How was I supposed to know what you were doing? Other than you were moonlighting for the sheriff, I didn't know what you were involved in."

"Don't get your dander up. I should have told you, but I couldn't. Cal reported the counterfeiting operation to Nevins long before you and I came down here. Only, she didn't provide a name. When Nevins learned we were going to be RVing, he asked me if I'd look into Cal's allegations," Mo said. "Then when she turned up dead soon after we got here, things became more serious. The more I talked to Stan about the flea market, the more I suspected Kat. I reported that back to Nevins yesterday. Undercover agents have been making purchases for the past week to gather evidence."

"Oh, no! Was Stan involved?"

Mo shook his head. "No, he just provided details about the flea market."

"Whew, that's good. We have to go after Kat."

"Woman, have you lost your mind? Nevins will take care of her."

I hobbled to the bedroom and retrieved the notes. "She's got Max!"

"I'm not even going to ask." He read the notes, and I registered his surprise. "You stay here. I'll meet Nevins at her RV."

"I'm going with you."

Mo put his hand on my shoulder. "You're not going anywhere."

"Try to stop me. Now saddle up the Jeep and let's go, because I can't walk so good."

Mo shook his head but helped me to the Jeep.

We'd barely fastened our seat belts when Sheriff Nevins pulled in behind us. Mo scrambled out to meet him, and I followed as quickly as my bum knee would allow. The look on Nevins's face made my stomach sink.

He clamped Mo on the shoulder. "She was gone when the feds showed up. We've got an APB on her."

"No!" I screamed. "She was just here. She has our dog. Mo, you have to do something."

"We're setting up roadblocks," Nevins said. "We'll get her."

CHAPTER TWENTY-FIVE

Stan, Sandi, Mo, and I sat in a booth at the Sunflower Café staring at menus. Both of our RVs were parked in the lot, and we were gathering for a goodbye breakfast before we hit the road. We'd not heard a word about Kat other than that the authorities believed she was still in the area. Despite his promise to stay until we found Max, Mo had convinced me we should head back to Pine Grove. The sheriff had promised to call with any news. Sandi and Stan were headed to the north shore of Lake Superior in Minnesota for a three-week stay.

It took everything I had not to cry at the table. We were leaving Max, but we couldn't do anything about it, no matter where we were.

"What'll y'all have?" Birdie asked, flipping her order book open and pulling a pen from her bird's nest of hair. "No cinnamon rolls today, but Lawton's got a pan of hot biscuits coming out of the oven any minute."

"Biscuits and gravy," Stan and Mo said simultaneously.

Sandi nodded in agreement.

"How about you, hon?" she asked.

My heart hurt too badly to eat. I couldn't bear the thought of Max being with Kat. I shook my head. "Nothing."

Mo rubbed my shoulders. "Bring her some biscuits and gravy too."

Birdie whistled to Lawton and held four fingers in the air. When he acknowledged the order, she shoved the pen back in her hair and leaned in. "Are the rumors true?" she asked. "About Kat?"

Sandi shook her head ever so slightly, trying to warn Birdie not to bring up the subject.

"Yes, they are," I said. "She's a murderer, a counterfeiter, and a dognapper."

Mo cut me a glance, and I averted my eyes to my phone, pretending to check for text messages.

Sandi patted my hand. "You'll get your dog back. Kat can't get far in that RV. She sticks out like a sore thumb. It's not like she can hide it."

I looked up, trying to put on a brave face in front of my new friend. "I hope so."

Thankfully, several customers walked in and Birdie had to leave to take their orders.

"I still don't understand how all this came together," Stan said. "Right underneath our noses. Mo, did Nevins let on to you what was going on?"

Stan had Mo in the hot seat now. Mo would not confide in him, so I was curious to see how he would handle the question. Back home, Mo had had to keep a lot of information from his best friend, Donny, but Donny, being director of the ambulance district, had his own privacy issues he had to follow. Both men stayed out of each other's business.

The sound of horns blaring, followed by the squeal of tires on asphalt and metal on metal, filled the café. Diners ran to the windows to see what caused the hellacious noises.

The café door burst open, and a man rushed in, shouting,

"There's been an accident on the highway. Someone call 9-1-1. An RV and a couple of cars collided, and people are trapped."

Mo signaled for me to make the call, and he nodded to Stan to join him. "Come on, man. Let's see if we can help until the paramedics arrive."

After calling for help, I joined Sandi at the window.

"That looks like Kat's RV," Sandi said.

"It can't be." I felt a glimmer of hope. "Why would she still be here?"

Several ambulances arrived and paramedics spread out. Mo and Stan had helped Kat out of her RV and had her seated on the side of the highway. Mo disappeared from my view. I threw open the door of the café and hobbled toward the scene, crossing my fingers and saying a prayer. When I got to the edge of the roadway, Deputy Beau blocked my way.

"You'll have to stay back, ma'am," he said. "We've got an investigation going on and need all civilians to stay on this side of the highway."

I continued forward, my mind set on one goal—finding my dog.

"Ma'am. I'm going to need you to stay here. It's not safe for you over there." He stood in front of me, blocking my view.

I side-stepped him only to be blocked again. "Get out of my way, young man."

"Ms. Modesky, please don't make me arrest you." He had a hand on his cuffs and a pleading look in his eyes.

"Mattie!" Mo's voice rose above the crowd that had gathered.

I looked around Deputy Beau and saw Mo carrying Max across the highway.

Tears flooded my eyes. "Is he okay?" I screamed.

Mo drew up alongside me. "He's fine. I couldn't find his leash and didn't want him getting lost in all the activity."

I buried my face in Max's fur and let the tears come as he

showered me with sloppy kisses and whined his relief. He wouldn't stay still, and I didn't care, but I squeezed him close and cried into his neck.

Stan joined us, leaving the paramedics and authorities to handle the accident. "That's a hell of a mess."

Mo nodded.

By now, Birdie and most of the customers had joined us in the parking lot. Lawton, oblivious to everything that had happened, stuck his head out the door and yelled, "What in the tarnation is going on? Birdie, I got four hot biscuits and sop up. Come and get them before they get cold."

Birdie, who was standing between me and Sandi, whispered, "Y'all wanna sit out here at the picnic table? Lawton's about to have a coronary. If you let those biscuits get cold, heads are gonna roll. And it's probably gonna be my head."

We lingered over breakfast long after Kat had been handcuffed and placed in the back of a patrol car. Even after the accident victims had been loaded into ambulances and the wreckage towed away, none of us seemed inclined to leave. Mo had retrieved another leash from our RV, and Sandi had brought out Scooter. The two dogs lay side by side, enjoying periodic pinches of biscuit or the occasional chunk of sausage and, for Max, endless head pats from me and Mo.

"After your trip home, where you headed next?" Stan asked.

Mo looked at me. "We have reservations in Wisconsin. There's a carnival that looks interesting. But, it depends on her. She's suffering from a bit of homesickness. Initially, I'd thought about the beach and getting in some ocean fishing. We're going to stick a bit closer to home. Besides, it might be too hot this time of year. Might want to save that for winter." Mo chuckled. "If she's still game."

"I'll have to think about it," I said. "If we do, and I'm saying a big *if*, my only requirement is to be home for the holidays. I want to decorate, go to Christmas parties with our friends, and have the kids home with us to celebrate. I don't even care if it snows."

Mo put his arm around me. "We can definitely do that."

"How do you all feel about Minnesota? We go to the same RV park every year. We'll be there for the summer solstice. It's really an amazing celebration. You could join us after Wisconsin," Stan said.

Mo's eyes lit up at the prospect. "What do you say, hon?"

I knew the look. After Wisconsin, we'd be heading to Minnesota. It was just as well. I liked Sandi, and I knew Mo like Stan, and despite their size difference, Max and Scooter had become fast friends. "Great!" I said.

"How's the fishing?" Mo asked.

"The place we stay is right on the shore of Lake Superior. The northern pike and smallmouth bass practically jump on your line. It'll be good eating. That's for sure." Stan signaled to Birdie. "Can we get a couple of coffees to go?"

"You think we can get a reservation or are we too late?" Mo asked.

"Shouldn't be a problem." Stan pulled a napkin from the holder. "You got a pen, Sandi?"

She fished one from her purse.

Stan pulled up a contact on his phone and jotted down the number. "Give Levi a call. He's the manager. He's a curmudgeon, but he's a good guy. Tell him you know me. He'll fix you up. If we're lucky, he'll take us out on the lake. He knows all the best spots."

Mo folded the napkin and put it in his pocket. "You okay with Minnesota after Wisconsin, hon?"

I nodded.

Sandi clapped her hands. "This is so exciting. I don't know if I can wait two weeks. Hurry. Okay?"

Birdie brought drinks to go for the entire table—tea for me and coffee for everyone else. When Mo and Stan started arguing over who was going to pick up the check, Birdie pulled the ticket from her order pad and tore it in half. "Last one is on me and Lawton, folks. Y'all travel safe and hurry back to see us."

We all stood in the parking lot for another half hour saying our goodbyes. Sandi and I hugged and wiped our eyes, each swearing we were having a bout with allergies, but we both knew we'd formed a lasting friendship, and saying goodbye, even for two weeks, was hard.

After letting Max and Scooter take a stroll around the parking lot, we said our last goodbyes and climbed into the RVs.

Mo fastened his seat belt and started the engine. "Homeward bound. Then on to a new place."

"Are you going to be working this next trip?" I asked. "Or are you retired this time?"

Mo winked. "I think the question really is, are *you* retired?"

I changed the subject. "It's a carnival. It'll be a fun vacation," I said. "Funnel cakes and fun houses, right?"

Max snuggled up between our seats, and we drove off, ready for our next adventure.

THE END

MATTIE'S STRAWBERRY SHORTCAKE DESSERT

Ingredients

1 prepared angel food cake torn into 1 inch pieces

2 lbs. macerated strawberries

1 large container whipped topping

Assembly

The presentation is pretty in a wide-mouth glass container such as a cracker jar. (You may need to adjust ingredients for the size of the jar.)

Add 1/3 of the angel food cake into the bottom of the jar.

Spoon 1/3 of the strawberries over the cake.

Top with 1/3 of the whipped topping.

Repeat layers until ingredients are gone.

Top with lid for storage or transport.

Refrigerate until served.

MATTIE'S WATERMELON FETA SALAD

Ingredients

1/2 tsp. salt

3 cups seedless watermelon, cubed (Slice top off watermelon and scoop out melon. Save shell to serve the salad in. Even up the bottom so melon shell sits level.)

1 cucumber, chopped

1/2 cup sweet onion, thinly sliced

1 cup crumbled feta

1/2 cup chopped mint

1/4 cup poppyseed dressing (more if desired)

Assembly (Make right before serving.)

Add the ingredients, mixing gently to incorporate. Serve immediately.

ALSO BY TRICIA L. SANDERS

Grime Pays Mystery Series

Murder is a Dirty Business

Between hot flashes and divorce papers, a middle-aged woman reconsiders her outlook on life when she butts heads with a hot detective during a murder investigation.

Death, Diamonds, and Freezer Burn

An unwelcome visitor, an unrequited love, and a dead body create chaos in Cece's plan for a productive summer.

Pensions, Tensions, and Homicide

A former friend, a runaway mother, and a dead body threaten to spoil Cece's low-key family Thanksgiving.

Mimosas, Magnolias, and Murder

Cece wants a day of self-care, mother-daughter time…and anything but her ex-husband's wedding.

The Mattie and Mo Mysteries

Hark! A Homicide (Prequel)

When a dead elf threatens to spoil Pine Grove's Christmas, being on Santa's naughty list is the least of Mattie's worries.

ABOUT THE AUTHOR

Photo Credit: Alecia Hoyt

Tricia L. Sanders writes cozy mysteries and women's fiction. She adds a dash of romance and a sprinkling of snark to raise the stakes. Her heroines are humorous women embarking on journeys of self-discovery all the while doing so with class, sass, and a touch of kickass.

Tricia is recent transplant to Texas, but she's still an avid St. Louis Cardinals baseball fan, so don't get between her and the television when a game is on.

A former instructional designer and corporate trainer, she traded in curriculum writing for novel writing, because she hates bullet points and loves to make stuff up. And fiction is more fun than training guides and lesson plans.

facebook.com/authortricialsanders
twitter.com/tricialsanders
amazon.com/Tricia-L-Sanders/e/B076NXMMFW
bookbub.com/profile/tricia-l-sanders

Made in the USA
Columbia, SC
20 October 2021